a day does not go by

a day does not go by

SEAN JOHNSTON

Nightwood Editions
Roberts Creek

Nightwood Editions
R.R. #22, 3692 Beach Avenue
Roberts Creek, BC
V0N 2W2, Canada

Edited for the house by Silas White
Typeset by Carleton Wilson
Cover painting "Relic," by Frances Ferdinands, acrylic on canvas, 1995, reproduced with permission of the artist.

We gratefully acknowledge the support of the Canada Council for the Arts and British Columbia Arts Council for our publishing program, and the support of the Saskatchewan Arts Board for this project.

Printed and bound in Canada

NATIONAL LIBRARY OF CANADA CATALOGUING IN PUBLICATION DATA

Johnston, Sean, 1966–
   A day does not go by

   ISBN 0-88971-190-9
   I. Title.

PS8569.O391738D39 2002   C813'.6   C2002-910999-X
PR9199.4.J63D39 2002

for Hettie & Gerry

Contents

We've never been sure of ourselves, have we,
    despite the beatings, despite the love, despite
governing our lives, being the only child
    moving into the green obscure forest

- John Newlove

this house

The mother wondered out loud all day long if you weren't all going to hell. No, you would say, to the first question of the morning. You could take lessons in this house. Intricate rules abused the rough men and kept them right.

Her movement and worry could heat the kitchen on its own. Stop moving, you would say on holidays, or during a day of heavy rain in the summer. Save yourself the trouble, just this once. She sighed and the idea itself renewed her.

You heard of wars, and other things. It's terrible, she said. You knew it was. Some day, everything will change, she said, and those that keep their mouths shut will babble with such fierce power the ones that couldn't shut up will have no choice. They that are fattened and gorged on money from blood will be sickened while the starved finally swallow their own pure hearts and grow to astounding heights. And the blind will see.

She couldn't read, so she made up her own stories. She knew there would come a day.

You took a chance doing the wrong thing there. You walk in one night real quiet and that illiterate old woman is up in the light of the stove right away saying you've got liquor on your breath. You stink. But maybe you'll get some sleep, you say.

You can't swing at her but you want to. She turns shaking her head, crying, what the bottle done to your uncle.

Next morning, before she asks, you know you're going to hell.

Look, none of this is going to happen, she says, without a gesture. You are not even listening.

Cripes, we're all tired, someone says. A young one, mind you, a grandson. He's the one who finally taught her to read. She wrote a long letter to you. You were gone then, but came back for the funeral.

It's not that I'm not dead, she says. I'm not arguing that. I feel okay though. This is fine. In the ground would be too much.

The women and the men in the tiny kitchen hold napkins of food and mutter how heavy the coffin was. She walks around oblivious over the pearly floor and smiling at the young ones. You can't catch her eye.

She doesn't see the bottle on the table. The rum in her kitchen doesn't make sense and maybe that's why no one talks to you. Sometimes your wife.

The people smiling are all good. The things they say you can't hear, but the people are all good. The one your brother married is sick but looks strong. Your sister is still hurt by the accident though she can walk fine. Your boy is stronger than you ever were.

The old woman will never look at you again. She sits writing at the table across and cannot see you. You may be thin air, fine, but she doesn't even hear the sound of glass when you almost drop the bottle pouring.

You can't read upside down. My oldest boy, she says, wanting to fight the hired man after his father died.

You were twelve that time and the man was across the yard. Before the old man died he told you look out for your mother and the simple math of it never made sense. The slow-moving big man died and the slight quick woman had too great a portion to bear.

The man wasn't asking much and neither was your mother. Nobody is ever asking much, but you heard her loud through the sun and the dust and it was enough. That's the time she rescued you.

She looks at you now and may speak.

You know she's not there. Your wife is beside you with her hand on your back. It's been too long, she smiles, to your brother in his worried old suit. He nods above his short fat tie and everyone smiles.

Come out tomorrow, you say. There are things to sort out.

Across the room your boy is sick of smiling. Don't say anything, you think. Don't joke about the coffin and don't tell the boy it gets better and don't touch a thing in this house.

nothing like this

When Wendell Sherman was in grade two, his parents could no longer believe in him. It was not their fault. Society went that way.

Ruth and Howard, the Shermans, were mystified at first. Their history set it up—the history before them. There had never been divorce in their family. They went to a counsellor called Judy, a young, thick woman right out of school and they sat there holding hands, ready to nod, ready to exclaim, ready to learn a way to go.

"What is this?" Judy said, holding a bright pink paper that had been folded twice.

"It's a notice," Howard said, then blushed. "Well, it came with a petition they were circulating at the school and we already . . ."

"Howard signed it," Ruth blurted, knowing this was evidence in her favour. She glanced quickly at her husband and then looked back at Judy to continue. "He signed my name to the petition, too. Then he dropped it off in the mailbox before I could see it. I don't think I would have signed. Maybe I would. I don't know. How could I know . . . he never let me decide!"

Howard squirmed and took a sip from his glass of water. He looked at Ruth and Judy, waiting for the tide to take them elsewhere. Yes, he had signed for her. He could see it was wrong but it was not malicious. If he waited and they kept speaking, he thought, they would get to an issue less embarrassing, more urgent. But they waited for him, silent.

"True," he said, nodding. "True. But in my defence, I thought it was nothing. I didn't read it myself. It was just one of those things. I think I was busy."

"Do you usually sign your name to things you don't read?" Judy asked him.

"Well, not usually, but . . ."

"But you did this time."

"I guess," he said.

Every time he said "I guess," Ruth and Judy would look at each other as if he was a child.

"Okay," he said. "Okay. I did. I don't guess, I know. I signed my name because a lot of things come up in this neighbourhood and you just don't know. It's nothing, almost every time."

"Well," Judy said softly. "Okay. I can see that. I understand. Sometimes these things just eat away at our time."

"Right."

"But you understand why Ruth may be hurt by this . . . " she looked at the pink paper.

"Sure I do. And I'm sorry." He turned to Ruth and said it again. "I'm sorry."

The paper explained it. The school asked that all students and teachers no longer refer to the boy Wendell Sherman, except as a myth. It explained that some parents had been complaining that if their children could not have their own beliefs spoken of in their school, except as myths, then they didn't want anything that was not commonly accepted, certifiable, verifiable, truth, to be spoken of to their children. Myths *become* truth, they said. It's time to take back reality. Wendell Sherman was blamed for everything, but none of the parents had ever seen him. He could not be real.

"Listen," Howard said. "Here's one. She—Ruth, I mean—brought this one home from the school and never even looked at it. It sat on the table for two days before I mailed it away."

"You're not supposed to say 'Here's one,' Howard," Ruth said. "It's not a competition. We're just talking and so—"

"She's right, you know," Judy said.

"Well it's just an expression," he said.

"Expressions come from somewhere, Howard," Ruth said, saying what she knew Judy was about to say.

Then their time was up.

On the way home, Howard said he didn't want to go back. He said he felt like Judy was against him. Ruth asked him to give it one more chance.

"I'm not talking about giving up," he said. "What about a different counsellor?"

"Well, let's give her one more shot. We've already started with her, you know, she's young and what not, up on all the latest and so on."

"But that's one of the things," he said, pulling into their driveway. "She invents things to prove the newest books and articles she's read."

"We'll try one more, okay?" Ruth said. "We've already paid for one more session."

They agreed and got out of the car. Ruth bent into the car to gather the groceries as Howard moved the bike from the walk into the garage and locked the garage door.

❧

Ruth Sherman was in the cookie business. She used to sell her mother's recipe, and just at her husband's bookstore. But the cookies took off. Everybody loved them. Howard, he didn't like them, but everybody else did.

Howard wanted a quiet store. The cookies brought in too many customers, and they weren't the kind that bought books.

"So put in some impulse things at the counter," Ruth said.

"Impulse things . . .?"

"Some tabloids even," she said, spooning some green beans onto her plate. "Order some tabloids like at the supermarket."

"Maybe if they weren't fresh," Howard said.

"What are you talking about? That's why people like them."

"I don't want all those people in my store. The people line up for the cookies, they don't come in to buy books and then the ones that do feel harassed."

"Not harassed," Ruth said, shaking her head. "They're not being harassed. Who's harassing them?"

The actual words didn't matter though. She knew

what he meant. Sometimes the cookie line made it so nobody could get in the store. You might think it was a cookie store.

She watched him as he looked at her. She chewed a piece of chicken. He drank from his glass of water and poured more. They stared at each other. It was how they came to conclusions, that's all. It was his store, after all. They were both unfailingly fair to each other.

When she stopped selling cookies at the store, a customer asked why, and Howard told him. The customer called Ruth and bought the recipe and the name off her. They made a deal—she got part of the business and she was the public head of the cookie company.

It wasn't just money she wanted. Her maiden name was Brand: Ruth Brand Cookies. It was a company with her name that sold her.

Howard got his bookstore back, Ruth made a little money . . . everybody was happy. They went on a trip to Montreal. They went to the Jazz Festival and things were never better. They loved each other during this time.

They never discussed children, really; one night it just must have happened. They thought she couldn't get pregnant, because she hadn't, ever. Not in the times he knew of, and not in the times he didn't know of, which consisted of one man.

Ruth had dated an older man. He was in his thirties and she was seventeen. Nobody knew but her and him and his mother. His mother never said a word. She was more ornament than human. She watched the TV and chain-smoked.

"This is Marilyn," he had said, pulling Ruth by the hand behind him. The old woman sucked hard on a mint, then lit another cigarette. Her wet eyes didn't blink. She didn't smile.

Three things she remembered about that man: the bowl of hard white peppermints on virtually every surface in his mother's house; the different name she was given each time they went there; her own disbelief at the boredom she felt—surely this was exciting stuff.

She didn't even remember his name. Not even the weight of his body. Just her hope that something would grab her, that something would make her want him, that something would happen that would explain how dull she felt.

So when Howard came to bed that night to simply offer praise, to thank her for their life together, to lie beside her looking at the ceiling and not touching, she had rolled over and pulled him to her. After the heat of the city and the smoke of the club, the cool bed seemed more imagined than real.

"You're a mirage," she said, the words too quiet for him to hear. Even she didn't hear them, though they felt like lovers' words in her throat, they felt like a thing she might say to a brand new man, and just then, after five years, Howard was.

Her eyes were wide open and his were closed. He smiled like a saint all night, as everything that did happen happened again and again.

One light buzzed outside their window. She felt like an ancient animal whose hunger would last forever.

❧

Wendell was born and when he was in grade two, something happened. It had started long ago.

Wendell was never a normal child. He was quiet and good, and average in appearance. He calmed people. He was too wise for a boy. If he had been more of an attention getter, they would have called him Wendy and beat him up.

There were other children at the school who may have been possible targets. For instance, a young boy, Chad Meuter, who was blue or green, depending on the light. His veins showed. He looked different, but none of the other kids picked on him. Why?

You walked up to him from the side, say, as he sat on the bench eating his sandwich. His thin legs were tinged blue at the knees—a subtle smudge that seemed to glow. He swung his legs and as you approached he turned and smiled with such confidence his slight body didn't matter. His will added twenty pounds to his frame.

He inspired confidence in the other children.

There was also Ruby Johnson, a big girl who wanted to be a boy. She smelled faintly of urine. Her clothes were always dirty and a bit loose. She had a bigger brother, or two, and she lived with them. She fought a lot. Her brothers never fought for her, but the idea was always in the back of the other kids' minds.

The main thing, though, was her heart—her origin and her heart's growth there. She defined, at this young age, the kids and what they thought. She was fine being a freak. So, you chose early on to be on Ruby Johnson's side, or against her.

The difference with Wendell Sherman is nobody noticed him, ever. The teachers never did; they would see marks for his work written in their books, but they wouldn't know how they had gotten there. They would hear students speak of him in the same hushed tones usually used for sex or religion and they understood him to about the same degree.

The other odd children stood out, but were allowed their space. Wendell was too invisible; if he ever made a gesture toward definition, nobody noticed. He mystified everyone with his ability to blend into the background.

ભૂ

Ruth saw the boy, Wendell. Deep down she believed in him still. But the mind can do funny things, the mind can be quite powerful. She had learned that in the therapy that saved her marriage. Howard had learned it too.

She explained it to a friend once. They were at a small Vietnamese restaurant, drinking too long after their meal. The sun was setting outside the glass front of the building. The green and pink linen on the tables was changing colour; everything was turning to grey. Ruth and her friend Mandy glinted in the half-light as they gestured with arms full of jewellery.

"I honestly don't know if I'm nuts, or what," Ruth said, leaning closer.

"Listen Ruth," Mandy said, lighting a slim cigarette.

"I mean, what if I'm just insane?"

"I said listen, Ruth."

"That's just what I need. To go insane."

"You just . . ."

"I'm a . . ."

"Just listen," Mandy said, taking an ice cube from her glass. "You're not insane, I said."

"I can't be insane," Ruth blurted. "I'm a cookie maven!" She smiled crookedly and raised her wine glass.

"A matron?" Mandy asked. "A cookie matron."

Ruth shook her head.

"You said . . ."

"What did I say?" Ruth asked. "That's what I said. A cookie matron, an old woman whose purity—"

Mandy laughed her own laugh, then staged a sublime smoking display, mixing the whorish with the elegant for the enjoyment of the empty tables around them. Her cigarettes had been taking the lipstick off her mouth all night. She had finally set the lipstick on the table with her change, reapplying it every time she stubbed out another butt.

"You said maven."

"I meant matron," Ruth laughed and slammed her ringed finger on the table. "What does maven mean?"

"I don't know."

"Then I could be right," Ruth said, suddenly serious.

"I don't think so."

"Maybe," she said, quietly starting to sob. "You never know when mistakes are right and what you meant is wrong."

Mandy moved her chair closer and put an arm around Ruth. She told her it was okay, though she didn't know what the matter was.

Ruth went into her quiet, tearful confession.

"I can't be insane. My cookie business is just me. It's all marketing."

"You're not insane, or—"

"I think I'm crazy," Ruth said, blowing her nose.

"Well . . ."

"We went to a therapist, you know," Ruth said, affecting a secretive posture and pushing herself a bit away from Mandy.

"You told me, of course."

"But we thought we had a kid once," Ruth said. "Me and Howard, we are some twisted people. We thought we had a kid."

"Wendell?"

"Yes, we called him that. Only it was a kind of delusion."

Ruth's hands covered her forehead. She took off her rings and laid them on the table by her crumpled napkin.

"I know it was a delusion, but I still see him sometimes. I still see him and I still talk to him. And he talks back."

Ruth knew it was insane. Everybody did. Mandy knew it too. But the alcohol was warming Ruth and she wanted to welcome it. Her son or not, if he was, then he is, she thought. Give this back to me.

What is more insane, after all? An old red-haired woman selling cookies on television, or a barren woman wanting to share her heart? What is crazy? Painting her face every day, or sharing a private moment with a young boy who made her very proud, whether he was a figment of her imagination or not?"

"I see him too," Mandy whispered.

Ruth ignored her. She was always going too far.

ℯꝋ

On a sunny winter day, Howard had gotten a phone call. His father was dying. His mother had died long ago, so long ago that he only knew her as an idea. He knew a mother was necessary, and he knew she had once lived, but he never knew her as a person.

It was the kind of day when all the seasons seem to exist together. The driveway was bare as he got into the car. The trees seemed on the verge of green, though you knew they weren't. The verge of it, the supposed imminent explosion of it, was in your mind, triggered by the smell of sweet things awakening to rot. Yet snow covered everything except the pavement, still. And summer, summer was in the sky.

Howard kissed Ruth goodbye and slid himself behind the wheel. She had told him she was pregnant, she had told him the morning after the night in Montreal. He had awoken to find her smiling at the ceiling beside him.

"I'm pregnant," she said.

He was sure she wasn't. So many times they had wondered, and it had never been true. The only difference this time was her happiness.

Now driving away to his father's death, Howard thought he saw a hint of what was missing before. She was radiant with the snow behind her reflecting light up to the cloudless sky. There was a round shape to her as she turned and the light housedress clung to her animal legs and she skipped back into the house.

It was possible. She was happy, and she had not been for ages. So . . . maybe she was right.

His father died slowly. He stayed with him for three months. There were stretches of days at a time when it was possible to believe he was already dead. He made no sound. He slept.

In lucid moments he would refer to conversations begun and ended years ago, as if they had a direct bearing on the day. Often they did. His old face was severe, but his rich, watery voice let Howard know his pleasure at his son's happiness.

As Howard stayed, nursing his father or listening to him, he came to accept that Ruth was right, that she was pregnant. When he thought of the child she carried, he thought of it as his son, though it could have been a daughter. He and his father spoke of the son. They came to depend on him.

Then, for all the slow building of his father's last days, and of their love and anticipation of the possible son, it happened suddenly.

Tuesday, his father died. Wednesday, Ruth had Wendell. Thursday, the funeral. Friday, a jagged Howard, empty and elated, drove home.

When he got back, Ruth looked the same as she ever

had, and he was puzzled, briefly, until they handed him the little boy. A boy from pictures, a baby from all the movies, a handsome, wholesome boy, who cried at all the right times and looked unreal in the crisp white bundle he slept in.

Bruce, a friend of a friend, had been looking after the bookstore while Howard was gone. He stayed on for a week or two after, just so they could get settled.

"Your homosexual friend," Ruth called him.

"He's not gay," Howard said. "Mark is. Just because they're friends . . ."

"It doesn't matter," Ruth said. "It's just funny that you don't know."

Howard didn't care. He looked at his boy and his wife and could not think of anything else.

***

Wendell watched as Howard approached him cautiously, and then sat on the couch beside him.

"Where do you go?" Howard asked him.

"I found a place in the school library," he said.

Howard looked at him and wondered how Ruth and he had ever gotten to this point. *What do you do there?* he thought. He meant to ask the boy, but could not speak out loud. Ruth may be home any second. That's the last thing he needed—for her to think he was crazy.

"I like to read books where nothing like this ever happens," Wendell said.

When the boy looked at him, his legs too small to

bend at the end of the couch, his hair uncombed and dirty, he couldn't think of anything to say.

"It's okay," Wendell said, scratching his nose. "I read all sorts of books. A lot of things happen. I know that. I just like the books where the people are happy. I don't believe them."

There was a key in the lock. Howard leaned over and hugged the boy, tightly, meanly. Time slowed like they were both dying, and he whispered to him.

"I still believe them," he said, knowing how pitiful it sounded. How pitiful it was—a man who believed, but could not act.

All through dinner he watched the boy go about his business in the living room. That was his rebellion—he didn't care if Ruth saw him steal glances at Wendell.

Once, when the boy was smiling into a book, he put his fork down and watched. He smiled too. He wanted Ruth to see him watching; he didn't care. But she was smiling at Wendell too.

The child looked up and wondered at this strange world. He could see the love in their eyes. He knew they meant better. He knew the world was caught in its own motion and he could not blame them.

∽

Ruth could not hold back.

"There's nothing either of us could have done," she said.

He watched his mother's face disappear. It melted.

She shrugged quickly and violently.

"What could I have done?" she asked, and her last wall fell down; she drew him to her. He sat on her knee, with his face against her wet cheek. She shook and rocked him.

The boy had not been touched for as long as he could remember. His mother whispered in his ear, smelling of hand lotion and soap. "You were the one thing holding us together. You were our boy. You were beautiful. Most people are surprised, but we never were—we *made* you. We *meant* to."

She held him tighter and he coughed.

"We both said it, later. That night, we both felt it. We willed it to happen."

She rocked her boy, letting herself fall into madness. She told him what they'd all learned in therapy: "We made you up—we wanted you so badly."

She understood at once, as she sucked snot back into her runny nose and swallowed it, that she was explaining to a figment of her imagination why she had ever believed in him.

She fell asleep saying to him, "Look. I don't care if I'm imagining you. You're here right now. Real or invented. I'm falling apart."

"Thank you."

here, and now

I didn't know Helen was dying when I saw the old man half-drag his friend toward the hospital. The sun was going down and the two men were just dark shapes in front of it. I hurried to them with a wheelchair.

They were burned from the sun and the big man pushing his friend in the chair had a bald and scabbed head. He looked too tired to think.

The emergency room was small and I stayed outside and had another cigarette while they answered questions to the nurse behind the desk.

After I finished my smoke I went in and asked the nurse if I could see Helen. She said no, again. Looking back, I might have known she was dying. I thought she was sick, but I didn't know she was dying. I thought, it's all right; this hospital is small and they might not have the staff to take me where I had to go, to where Helen was.

Sometimes it doesn't make sense, what a guy thinks. Sometimes it just doesn't make sense. Everyone comes to Banff to hike and to ski and to camp, but we were just driving through. We were on our way to Vancouver, to see some of Helen's friends from college. We were just married and the trip would merge our lives even further—it would thread our pasts together somehow, me meeting her old friends. At least that's what she said. I believed her, or I believed that's what it might do for her. I didn't always understand her, but most of what she meant made sense.

One morning, she was looking out across a fallow field toward the dawn and said sometimes she felt so close to something larger, she couldn't think of another name for it but God. I never liked to talk about those things. I'm afraid of many things.

"You know what I mean?" she asked.

I looked at her and smiled.

"I mean, here we are, and how else?" she said. She had a way of stretching that seemed like luxury. She would stretch right into me.

"I don't know," I said. I didn't. I don't. She seemed a little hurt, so I pulled her closer. I loved her. I know that.

"I don't know every second of every day," she whispered. "But here, and now, I know. A day does not go by without my thanking God I have you."

The woman sometimes made me want to weep from tenderness, she said so many things I would have said but didn't know how.

And now in the hospital, the nurse wouldn't let me see her. It was probably the doctor, I guess. I don't know. So I sat down in the plastic chair and flipped through an old magazine. I wasn't worried, which, like I say, was because I didn't know.

I looked for the old man. What the hell? I thought.

He's in there with his buddy but I'm out here waiting to see my wife. I was old enough to know better, even then, but I hung onto the word like it could keep me from ever being hurt. She's my *wife*. That woman there, the one with the slender body I was still surprised to hold, the one with the nose you might think too large until that elastic smile wrote her face back into joyous proportion and love was the only way out—that woman, she's my wife.

I was about to jump to my feet and shout, but then I saw the old man at the pay phone just inside the door, just as there was an answer at the other end.

He was tanned and burned and his bald head was ringed with a thin line of dirty hair. He held the bridge of his nose and leaned against the wall by the phone with his eyes closed, then opened them and said "Hi."

"I know," he said. "I know."

The room was so small I had to hear him, but I tried to look away. I tried not to listen. The nurse at the desk was busy writing something.

"I know, dear. I've got to stay with Alex."

He listened for a moment, then said, "Either he's got no way home or I've got no way home."

"He broke his fucking ankle—sorry dear."

He closed his eyes again and turned to lean against the wall. He was so large it seemed he was supporting the building, more than resting against it.

"No. I know. I've got to stay here."

"I know," he said, nodding.

Then his eyes were looking right at me, I thought. I held the magazine up in front of my face, but I couldn't help looking over it, now and again.

"Well, let's not . . ."

"Okay dear but you've got to . . ."

"No, I know. I know, but you can't think I planned this. The kid could have been fucking killed! I'm not leaving him out here to find his own way home."

His thick fingers relaxed on the phone then tightened again.

"What?!" He pulled the phone away from his head and stared at it for a second.

"Look, I'm here at the hospital in Banff, in the emergency room. We were working in Canmore and—"

His face was blank. He seemed like he might drop the phone, like his whole body might give up and collapse. I raised the magazine again and tried to read what was on the page. It was something about growing herbs on your apartment balcony.

"You don't believe me," he said.

For some reason, then, he must have realized I was in the room too. I don't know why. I felt him staring at me.

"Wait a minute," he said into the phone, then put his hand over the mouthpiece and gestured toward me. It took me a minute to realize he wanted me to come over. He waved more frantically, and I stood up.

"Buddy, listen, do me a favour?" he said, holding the phone out to me. "Tell her where I am. She doesn't believe me."

I reached half-heartedly for the phone. He looked embarrassed and added "Please," and "Sorry."

I said hello and waited. There was nothing at the other end. I looked at him and finally a voice on the other end asked, "Who is this?"

"James," I said. "I, uh, I'm here at the hospital." There was silence, and I thought I should say more.

"My name is James Cowles and my wife's sick."

Silence.

"Uh, we were on our way to Vancouver and—"

"Who is this?" she asked. She was accusing me of something. And before I could answer again she screamed at me "Is that you, Rick?" and I was stunned back into silence. She was crying.

"Why don't you let him tell his own lies, Rick? He's never home and I've had it, you bastard! You know he's fucking that little tart, you know he is, and now you're lying for him. Where are you?"

She went on and on, talking in the short bursts and deep breaths of someone really crying. I watched the old man, and he watched me like I was some goddamn judge or something. She told me he was sleeping with someone from work. She said he was never home. I didn't know what to say and I was about to hand the phone back to him but the look on his face—I don't think he could have said anything anyway.

"Please, ma'am," I said. I don't think I had ever used the word ma'am before in my life. I don't think I've used it since. "My name is James and I've never met your husband before. I'm waiting for my wife and I can tell you we're in Banff right now but I don't know anything about anything else."

The old man slid down to the floor with his back to the wall and put his head in his hands. He shook a little, and I think he was crying, but I couldn't hear—all I could hear was the woman on the other end of the phone sobbing and whispering the question, over and over again in my ear, "Why are you lying to me?"

I asked her name. She said I knew her name. I said I didn't. I asked her to humour me. I said I was sorry, because I didn't know what else to say. The man at my feet was still looking down, still shaking a little.

"Gail," she said quietly.

"Gail, I'm sorry. But I don't know what to tell you. I came here with my wife Helen and she's sick and I haven't seen her for what seems like forever. We were supposed to be going to Vancouver. It's our honeymoon."

I thought that summed it up and I was ready to hand the phone to the man on the floor, who had just sniffed and was getting ready to stand up. He had a sheepish smile on his face. I think he thought everything would be okay now. But the silence on the other end seemed to ask for more. I don't know.

"I think she's dying," I said into the phone and then heard her hang up as the man held his hand out for the phone. I didn't think my wife was dying, and I don't know why I said it.

"She hung up," I said, shrugging and trying to smile as I handed him the phone. Then I hurried back to my seat and sat down. He sat down beside me.

"Sorry," I said.

He shook his head dismissively and stared straight

ahead. It seemed like a very long time, then he shifted in his seat and straightened a little.

"What did she say?" he asked quietly, still looking forward.

"Well, I don't know . . ."

"Look," he said, turning to face me, "It's a shitty situation to be in, I know. It was stupid of me to do, ask you to do that"—he took a deep breath and let it out slowly— "but I didn't know what to do. I don't know what she thinks. I don't know a goddamn thing in that woman's head."

It was silent and I looked up at the nurse. She was looking at me, then looked down.

"She thinks you're sleeping with someone from work," I said as softly as I could. "She thought I was one of your friends, making something up to cover for you. I told her my wife might be dying."

"She's in bad shape?"

"Well, she was crying pretty good."

"What is it?"

"No. Your wife, I mean. She was crying on the phone. I think my wife's alright."

"Oh," he said. "So she thinks I'm fucking Trina."

"I guess."

"I don't know what the hell to do."

He told me she was the one who had cheated on him, but he loved her, so he never let on he knew. He knew the affair was over and he knew it hurt her to remember. He couldn't bring himself to say anything, but he thought everything was over—she had stopped going out all the time, even though he worked out of town a lot and wasn't usually home during the week. He told me he trusted her again. But he didn't know where she got whatever it was she thought.

He talked fast and quietly, shifting his feet in front of him and shaking his head from time to time. Then he looked at me again with red eyes.

"Your wife will be alright?"

"Yeah. I don't know, but I'm pretty sure." I didn't know. I don't know why I was so sure everything would be alright. I told him how it hurt to see her in pain and he nodded. I told him about our trip to Vancouver, to see her friends. I told him again I knew she was alright. But of course I was worried, I said.

"You should be with her," he said.

"They won't let me."

He nodded and stroked his head with one hand. The light in the hospital was not real, I know, but it still felt like it must be morning.

"You should be with her," he whispered.

"Hey, I told you—they wouldn't let me. I've been asking."

"If it were my wife dying, I wouldn't ask."

"She'll be alright, I told you! I don't even know your goddamn name. Why the hell are you sitting here telling me what to do when you . . ."

I stopped. He looked at me like some big dumb kid, hurt. Not mad, just hurt. He said his name was Tom.

"Sorry," I said. Sitting in the waiting room, two tired strangers apologizing to each other. It's not right.

"Anyway," I said. "She'll be okay."

"Yeah."

He stood and went to the fountain. He took a drink of water and splashed some on his face, then wiped it on the sleeve of his shirt.

"She'll be alright. They know what they're doing," he said. His face was still wet around the edges. One small shock of hair at his forehead curled in the shape of a *c*.

"Yeah," I said.

We smiled at each other.

"Want a smoke, Tom?"

He shook his head. "Go ahead. If they call for you, I'll come get you."

It might have been winter outside, for how cold it had gotten. I know that's an exaggeration. I know it is, but that's how I remember it. It was that cold, but there were still mosquitoes and little flies swarming and biting me, as I paced back and forth in front of the door, smoking like it was a job.

Now and then I looked in and saw Tom sitting on the edge of his seat with his head in his hands. How do you hurt such a big man?

I was about to come in, once, but I saw him get up and go to the phone. She was having none of it, I could tell by his expression. It was exactly like the other phone call. The exact same thing. Then he took the phone from his ear, looked at the nurse and pointed back over his shoulder toward me.

Tom said something else into the phone and hung

up, then took a step toward me before he realized I was watching him. He waved me into the hospital, then walked into the bathroom.

The nurse told me I could see Helen.

I didn't find anything out that night. I held her hand and she said she was feeling better. I told her I'd been worried but that I knew she would be alright. She said she knew. I told her about Tom, but I must have been whispering.

She would ask the same questions over and over again: How old is Tom? How old is his wife? How long have they been married?

She said he seemed like a nice guy.

"He is," I said, but I didn't know.

She shook her head. She couldn't believe any of it, lying there half-asleep, her hand in mine. She would wake suddenly sometimes, like she was surprised.

"You're still here," she would say, then sleep again.

some words, she said

I walked quick by the hippie chick putting dirt in clay pots. This town's an asylum. Her hands were red from the cold. I wanted to get by her before she smiled. She had six clay pots and they were almost full. I've seen her everywhere.

I just wanted a drink of water. This town's all dust. It's barely spring, but one day of sun brings dust. She looked up and smiled. Every pot was filled. She digs all the time. I think it's her job. I smiled at her and she went back to her work, putting the full pots back onto her little red wagon.

Maybe she's not a hippie. I don't know. I kept walking and I kept walking home. I was sweating. I was dressed too warm. Two fat men were on the sidewalk in front of me. They wheezed when they laughed. One called the other a fucking so-and-so. It made me smile. They were red too, like the hippie chick's hands. It must be cold in the earth.

I had to stop. The fat men said hello. How do you do? I suppose they said. Fine, fine. Sure, sure. Such and such, one said. They nodded and wheezed. Nice enough fellows.

The hippie chick was pulling her wagon behind me.

Up the street, she lived in a house. I heard her behind me, her noisy wagon rolling on concrete. This town's all red. The wagon, the faces, the hands, are all red. I loosened my tie. Well, yes, mister; you, and you there, I said.

Even so, said the hippie chick, smiling all the while. She was beside us. Beside me and the fat men. They parted to let us pass. I nodded as the hippie chick spoke and we walked. I was going to get a drink of water. She must have been going home.

The policeman asked me a question. Well, is this dirt right? or something. Is this the right dirt? The hippie chick had many colours of clothes on. Some words, she said, nodding her head while the little cop poked the dirt with a stick. He had a dog with him. A police dog.

The dog was all wet and it smelled. It looked at me embarrassed. I just wanted some water. The dog rolled his eyes while the cop spoke. Yessir, I said, even so. I pulled out some papers and pointed some words to his stick. He might need glasses soon. There was something about him.

You gonna let the hippie chick go with the dirt? I asked. And the man who was a cop smiled at the woman who was smiling at him. It's good work, he said. Good dirt.

I'd like a glass of water, I told him. His dog was with me, the dog was thirsty. It's not that hot, the little cop said. Where's the big cop today? This town's got two cops. One little, one big. It's barely spring, he said.

He hit me twelve times on the shoulders and neck with his club. I guess I deserved it. This town is not right. I should move to another town, somewhere there's no hippie chick slowing me down. Such and such, I said. The little cop nodded and I kept walking.

You and your dirt, I said. I just want a drink of water.

It's not that hot, she said in a good little cop voice. She smiled. I could tell she smiled but I looked straight ahead. Where's the big cop she said in a good thirsty voice. I knew she was smiling again.

This town's full of holes. The hippie chick stopped by my house and filled six on my lawn. She took so much time, licking her fingers and thumbing through dirt like it was a book. Her skirts were all coloured around her as she knelt on the ground.

I brought her a glass of water when she was done. She drank and looked at her empty wagon.

Your neck and your ears are as red as that wagon, she said. So on and so forth, I said, taking the glass from her.

the reporter and the reporter

He covered wars the best he could. Words hung in the air like murdered fish, coveted for their precision.

She said she didn't like magic realism. He said the world decides.

Literature is one thing. She said you can't talk about books. He said I walked out of the fog one morning and slipped on a bloody ear. I don't know where it came from.

She imagined a tub of water, that's where her fog came from. She was cleansed. He said you've been there too.

I don't think my heart could break if magic were real. He said your breaking heart invents it.

Stop. This will be the end of us. I need a way out of here. They both got on the bus and a boy without hands smiled at them, talking quickly.

Her notebook was full. His face could not get enough of her sad look. He was in love. Blisters broke on his heel when the bus rocked to a halt.

The boy shook his head. No, no. Cannot be, he said.

They pretended to not know his language. Passengers spilled off the bus and made their way angrily in all directions.

They saw the boy among them, holding a fighting chicken in his abbreviated arms.

Where is your magic? she asked, striding to the front of the bus. He followed her because of his love.

A plastic flower of red grew on the seat behind the stopped driver.

We need a cab. The frantic street agrees.

the whole time I was here

There was no sign of a fight. The man just lay there, not breathing. Or breathing very shallowly. She had not checked.

But then the live man showed up. He asked her name.

"Beth."

He began to sweat as soon as he stepped from his car. "What is this?" he said.

"I don't know. The man has been lying here for as long as I can remember."

It was a slip; she meant as long as she had been there. How long was that? It had been only ten minutes. Maybe five. She wasn't sure. She thought he was dead and time moved slowly when she found someone dead.

"He's not dead," he said, looking up at her from where he knelt by the man. The man on his back was not wearing a shirt, just greasy jeans. The blond hair on his chest was not holding sweat, like it would if he were living.

"What happened?" she asked as the man stood up.

"I don't see any blood. I don't understand. Do you have a phone?"

"No."

The man looked to the sky and the sun stared back. The wind blew briefly and gave them a moment of relief and then it was gone. Her skirt settled back around her legs and she was hot again.

"My name is Jeff."

She almost laughed but then remembered the dead man.

He's not dead, she told herself. She laughed.

"I don't understand," he said, wiping the sweat from his forehead. "What's so funny?"

"Nothing. I'm sorry. I know he's in trouble. Is he still breathing?"

The man bent down to look closely. "It's tough to tell. I think he is, but it's very faint."

They looked at each other as Jeff stood up. He looked up again at the sky. A slow bead of sweat rolled from his sideburn along the edge of his jaw, then down his stretched neck.

"What are you doing here, Jeff?"

"What do you mean?"

She didn't know what she meant.

"I mean, what should we do?"

"I don't know. You don't have a phone? No, I already asked that. I wonder . . ."

"I'm not from here. Are you?"

"No."

"I wonder how far it is to the next town."

Jeff said he didn't know.

"I suppose we should drive him to the next town."

"I don't think so," he said. "I don't think we should move him."

Beth looked all around her. A desert or a prairie, what's the difference when there's no rain? She was glad Jeff had shown up but she thought live men should be more active, more sure of what to do.

Still, as soon as he'd shown up, as soon as there was a live man there, she felt better. Dead men gave her the creeps.

Where can the answers be, with a dead man staring at the sky incapable of asking anything? With the sky draped over the world and the prairie stretching forever, not only are you alone, you know you are alone. You can see there is no one all around you, in every direction.

Unless you count the dead man: a sentence fragment; a verb lying awkwardly in the desert, understood by no one. Dust heating itself until the sun and earth are one. Say the verb quickly and it shakes like a flesh doll; a garish display of human insolence; a B-movie actress beating at death's chest before succumbing to the comfort.

She doesn't entirely discount him and that's why dead men give her the creeps.

"What?" Jeff asked. "Do you have an idea?"

She was smiling to herself, as she looked around, from the sky to the ground. "No."

She stopped smiling and sat down in the dead grass. The man still looked dead to her.

"I think he's dead," she said.

"Well . . ." he said, looking first at his car, with the door still open, then at the man on his back, then at Beth, as she sat on the ground with her hands holding her ankles.

"How long have you been here?"

He walked to his car and shut the door.

"You asked that already," she said.

"Oh. Sorry. How long was it again?"

"What does it matter? There is this dead man"—she stood and turned toward him—"and you have a car and there must be something we can do."

"Well, I don't think we should move him is all." Jeff looked at her timidly.

"You don't think we should do anything, do you?"

"I don't know."

"Jesus, Jeff, we've got to do something. If you're going to stand and ask me the same questions over and over again you might as well go on about your business. Where were you going?"

"I don't know." He didn't know. He was driving, just driving.

She laughed and turned away. She ran a hand through her hair, then decided she would keep walking. After all, to her, the man was dead. You cannot save a dead man. There is no help to be given.

"Wait," Jeff said, and she felt his hand on her bare shoulder. "Where are you going? I can give you a ride."

"You can't give me a ride—you have to figure out what to do about this dead man."

"He's not dead. Plus, you found him, so really, he's your responsibility."

"But you don't think he's dead, Jeff. I do. A dead man cannot be saved so I have no responsibility to this dead man I found. You do, because you came upon a live man. You see?" Beth asked, smiling, with both her palms out, shrugging.

"I don't think so. We both have a responsibility."

When he looked at her, she knew he was all edges, she knew he could not take much. He was exasperated and she was afraid he might cry. She didn't want that. She didn't know which was worse, a silent dead man or a crying live one.

He wiped sweat from his forehead and sighed as he looked at the naked earth around them, then stared again at the sun. Sweat gathered at the collar of his shirt.

Who wears a tie to an argument over a dead man with a strange woman in the desert? she thought, and reached to loosen it. He flinched and turned quickly with fear in his eyes. His body's strength shot through the dark tie to her. It moved her like electricity.

"Sorry," she said, but didn't let go. "I just thought you should loosen this tie, or take it off. It's so hot out."

"Oh," he said, and watched her as she loosened his tie, then pulled it over his head with a shrug.

"If anything," she said, swinging the tie in circles beside her, "the dead man over there should have a tourniquet, not you—this was keeping the blood from your brain."

He stared dumbly at her.

"A dumb joke," she said.

He forced a chuckle, then sat with his back against the rear tire of the car.

She sat down beside him. With the sun so high, there was little shade by the car. He leaned back and looked at the sky with his eyes squinted against the sun.

"You can't get away from it," he said.

"We need to do something," Beth said, laying a hand on his shoulder.

"There's no point," he said. "You're probably right. He's already dead. He was dead the whole time we've been here."

"I think so," she said, nodding. She saw his whole shirt was wet with perspiration. The dark circles of his nipples were plain through his white shirt.

"Well, he's been dead the whole time I've been here, anyway," Jeff said.

"But you mean you think I found him alive?" she asked, standing.

"I'm just saying I don't know." He held his hand above his eyes to look at her. The sun was strong and all he saw was a silhouette. The shape of her stood still in front of him and said nothing.

"Hey," he said. "Sit down again. I can't see you." She didn't move and so he said it again.

"I can't see you," he said, "and I'm sorry. I don't know what is wrong."

"Well, you said this man died while I was here— that it's my fault." She sat beside him.

"I didn't mean that. I just meant I cannot know. Strictly speaking, I can't, right?"

"Well," she said, "I don't know about all that. When I found him he was dead."

"I believe you," he said. "But I don't know what happened. I can't."

"Jesus, Jeff, that makes no sense—"

"Never mind," he said, "that's just the nature of knowledge. And—"

"And so I wouldn't understand, right?"

"I didn't say that," he said, turning to look at her. Her eyes were intent and unblinking. She raised her arm and his hand jerked up in front of his face. When she scratched her head, he rubbed at his sweaty forehead and blushed. Why had he thought she would hit him?

"You think I'm stupid because I'm pretty," she said, pushing her hair behind her ears.

"I never said you were pretty," he said, laughing. His body shook as he watched her glare at him, then he stood to regain some control. He took a breath and stopped laughing.

"I'm sorry," he said. "It just seemed a lot funnier than it probably is."

She stood too.

"I just don't like to be insulted."

"No. I know. You're a beautiful woman. I can see that."

"That's not it, you idiot!" she screamed.

He watched her in silent wonder. Her fists were balled tight at her sides and she looked at the ground and took a deep breath. When she spoke again her words came out measured and controlled.

"I just am not an idiot," she said. "I just don't think"—he was about to speak but she held a hand up and he stopped—"I just don't think because I don't believe in a lot of philosophical junk that means I'm stupid. It doesn't even mean I don't understand it. I knew a guy once who had all these theories. Every day there was a new one. For instance, he might say this is all a day-dream in the mind of some greater being."

"But is the being daydreaming, is he one of us?" he asked.

"I don't know. The specifics don't matter. None of it matters. You and I are here. The dead man is here. Who cares?" She slapped herself hard on the forehead.

"See?" she said. "Me! If I am imagined, it doesn't matter because I am right here, as if I am real."

He didn't say anything, and she sat down against the car again.

"According to this guy I knew we might all be just characters in a book."

Sitting down beside her, he shook his head.

"That makes no sense," he said quietly.

"Of course not, but it could be true."

He pulled his knees up to his chest and laid his head on them.

"What about the dead man?" he said, closing his eyes.

"Well, the dead man might be a character that's not being used right. What if the reader isn't paying close attention? What if you and I know that dead man and the reader has forgotten the connection? What if this book means . . ."

"I'm so sick of books," he whispered into his folded arms.

"What?"

He raised his head and looked at her. His cheeks were wet and his face looked fluid, like every part of it could go its own way. Then it came back to the straight, lined face of the man he was.

"I'm just so sick of books," he said, and she stared at him, waiting for more.

"Well, I just don't know why I'm here," he said. "I just got in my car and started driving. I am sick of books and Jen, that's all she does is read, I think."

She gently touched his shoulder. He sobbed and hugged his body into a ball again. She put her arm across his shoulders and leaned her head on him.

"So, you . . ." she said, rubbing his back.

"So, if this were a book, if you and I were characters in a book, then we would fuck and this dead man would be your husband and we would feel bad later, for him and for Jen, but we would carry this ridiculous muted love to the end of our days and your husband, and my wife, they might be terribly hurt but you and I, we're the heroes of this book and—"

He coughed and snorted, then pulled a hanky out of his pocket and cleaned his face. He seemed more angry than sad, now.

"I just mean in books, good people are mocked. Everything immoral is normal. Nothing is wrong. Everyone does it."

"Does what?" Beth asked.

"Anything they want. Nobody judges them. Their affairs are described like a bunch of trees in fall, or a desk or a card table . . ."

"But they're just books," she said. "They're just fake like movies. Like bar stories or whatever."

"I know," he said. "It's just that she reads these books. She reads them and I hear her talk about these people and she likes them. She tries to get me to read them too, and sometimes I do—so I can talk to her about them, and because they have made her so happy."

He looked at her and shook his head.

"Never mind. It's stupid. It's just that she likes these characters, she has real affection for them. And they have done the most hurtful things."

She rubbed his back, leaned forward and kissed his cheek. He stood, then so did she.

"I think we should do something," she said.

He stretched, watching her. Her back was to him and she watched the dead man. He felt as if he'd been sleeping for days and couldn't help but smile as his relaxed body settled after stretching.

"I only told you that," he said. "I only told you because that's why I don't know where I am. That's why I wasn't going anywhere, in particular. We had a fight and I wasn't thinking, really."

"It doesn't matter, Jeff," she said, walking over to the dead man.

They stood and stared at him, she on one side and he on the other. The sun had moved while they were here. It was still high, but it shone on Beth's back. She watched the dead man and Jeff watched her. Her blonde hair hung straight down at the sides of her bent neck. She looked to him as if she had stepped from an air-conditioned theatre, she was so clean and sharp. He felt smudged and oily in this desert, or prairie, or wherever it is they were.

The dead man sighed and Jeff looked down just as he opened his eyes.

"We better take him to the next town," Jeff said. "I think you're right."

"I know," she said.

They helped the dead man to his feet and he sat in the back seat as they drove. It took an hour, but nobody said a word the whole way.

once took a room

We didn't know if we'd see each other again. My girl was leaving. I said I'll come get a job out there. She said okay but we both didn't know.

That night was long. We held each other like corpses; we didn't know what to do except to keep quiet and think I love you.

The next days were dark and cold.

I called one night and said I can make something up. There's money out there, I said. She knew. I said I'm not afraid of hard work. She knew that too. She said she knew.

The town already looked old to me as I walked to the depot. I was caged on that bus for three days.

In the new dirty city, with everyone rushing, I saw an old building.

The apartment manager asked what I did.

"I'm making up a superhero," I said. "I'll write a comic and draw a great costume and sell the rights to the movie."

"What do you do now?" he asked.

"I build telephones two blocks away."

"I know the company. Okay, seventy-two dollars a week. Do you want it?"

I took it and it wasn't bad. It was a new city with

money. I'd get a job somewhere. The place down the street was hiring but I didn't know anything about making phones.

The only trouble was it was small, with no window. But that's okay because I chain-smoked but I was young and me and my girl, we had a new life to begin.

I called her up and I talked to her mother, then she came on so I said you know I've got a new place and the next thing I knew I was combing my hair and buzzing her up.

Let's go, my boy, she said to me—we're buying new shoes and then having a drink. Eat a sandwich then let's go to that clean place on the corner.

I don't have any food, I told her and she smiled and said that's okay. She came right up and we put our arms around each other and her hands were cold on my back. Her tongue was wet and cool in her smile.

I said it's a cold fall out there anyway and this is my first night here with my girl. She said you're right and we've got a long time. That's when we laid ourselves down in that new warm apartment, we laid ourselves down in our coats and our sheets.

It's so warm, we said, and watched each other make love to the other in this new city in this new time and it was warm and it was all out in front of us.

Thank you, I said, and I felt embarrassed. Thank you, she said, over her shoulder. We thanked the whole room and she pulled a bottle of wine from her pack.

This is it, my boy, she said, you've escaped the new shoes but this is the drink.

And we drank.

spiders door to door

Nobody can tell a used spider. You sell them new. Even if they're not. The rough formula, an outline of the rules of thumb, could take forever.

Read the customer as they come to the door in housecoat or whatever. Is this an exotic spider today? Or is this a regular, working spider? Is it imported? Is it domestically and organically grown?

What sort of webs does she envision? This one can take a while. This one can last ages.

Fiction, all of it.

Who wants a spider?

You leave, usually, and go down to the donut store. You have a coffee with the regulars.

"Way too many questions," someone mutters. "Always with the questions. I should bother him all day and then he'd get the picture. A man can't work with that over-the-shoulder business. Bottom line, the job gets done."

You commiserate. You know how it is.

"Fucking quotas," you chime in, and they notice you for the first time that morning.

"Cripes, Roy, how'd you sneak in like that?"

Always the same questions. You're not up to it. You ignore it. The woman behind the counter brings you a coffee and a plain cake donut.

You tell her thanks. Of course her name's Rita. It's perfect. She owns her own house by the money from this miserable job, if you can believe. She smiles at you, her hair just right. Her dull yellow uniform fits just right; either her body or the cloth has made some adjustments.

The others go on around you. They have names like Ned and Joe, Sam and Bud. They try to involve you.

"Roy, you gotta take her up on it."

"Take her up on what?" Bud cuts in, before you can say a thing.

"That fucking time she—"

"Never mind that time, I still don't believe it. She's something, and who the fuck is Roy?"

You let them go on. Bud's sweet on Rita and you don't want to let him in on it. You don't want to let him think Rita's no good but Jesus look at her. She's almost fifty, for sure, she's almost fifty and it's not that she wears too much makeup or dresses too young but the lazy way she flirts with the Buds and Neds is pathetic.

She's over at the end of the counter now. The far end, away from all of you, and Bud's talking about going ice fishing this winter. He just bought a new trailer. He's talking about getting out on the lake for a month and Jesus he's a big man and you don't want to think of him wrapped in blankets and parkas and drinking with his cousin in some little box. What do they get on about? How do they live? And even with the fish and the smoke and the whiskey a month is too long for grown men to have things to say to each other.

He's going on about it but you know his heart's not in it. He's checking down to the far end of the counter where Rita's laughing with some new guy, some stranger.

Late one afternoon you'd been the only one in there. You'd been there after a day and Rita came to the end of her shift and put her hand on your shoulder as she left.

"See you next time, Roy," she said.

You were too busy thinking. An impossible box of spiders sat in the back seat of your car and you hadn't sold a thing in over a week. So you didn't say anything. She stood there one moment, with her hand on your shoulder. The sunlight through the glass walls of the shop weakened, as wooden a movement, and as slow, as the notched ticking of a clock. But she left before you could speak.

You stop and stretch once you leave the donut store. As your body relaxes you see Rita at the bus stop in front of the strip mall. She's in her uniform. Some of the younger ones change for the ride to and from work. A child waiting for the bus says something and Rita half-smiles at him, but you can see she's not into it. She's got no strength left.

"Have a good night, Rita," is what you should have said. Or something like Bud would say, something suggestive, something verging on lewd but just to let her know she's okay. Just to let her know there's something about her and you noticed. But you're no good at those things.

"Rita!" you yell, waving. Your smile isn't forced

because you know she's been nice to you all this time but it's an effort for her too, sometimes. You appreciate it.

So when she walks over you feel obliged. You just meant to let her know you mean well. You just wanted to cheer her up, but when she walks over you offer her a ride, not knowing what else to do.

Close up, she's happy again.

But nothing happened. You gave her a ride home and you thought she was nice but you knew just by looking she wasn't for you. She spread out on the seat and looking at her sideways at a red light you saw up close the pinched insincerity of her eyes when she smiled. Never mind, she's a good person.

It's just that Bud thinks you've got a thing for her. He thinks she's got a thing for you. None of it's true but you've got the kind of voice where what you say comes out wrong, where people take whatever meaning they want.

Nothing against Rita, she's fine for Bud. You've got other fish to fry.

This one you saw this morning, she's the one for you. Bud can have Rita and you'll tell him so as soon as he's done about ice fishing. You'll tell him the woman you saw is the one for you.

She came to the door from outside. Her husband is in a wheelchair and she rolled him up behind you while you waited at the door with a shoebox under your arm.

"Can I help you?" he said, as you turned. She stood behind him, elegant and tanned. They both had dark glasses on.

You could tell he couldn't move his body. You could tell he was older than her. Mr. and Mrs. Winter. She smiled when he told jokes.

The whole time, she said nothing. She lowered her head once to brush off an insect that she felt on her leg. Her sunglasses slid down her nose. Her eyes were dark, the whites clear and fresh. She paid no attention but just by her shifting legs under her light dress, you could tell. She was antsy. There was something she wasn't getting from the old man.

You slipped a card into his shirt pocket, but you were looking at her. When you watched them move into the house, she didn't look back, but she leaned forward over him, what for you can't imagine. Her right foot left the ground slightly and she kicked her sandal off, girlish. A thin silver anklet caught in sunlight. She closed the door behind them without looking back.

The old man must go to bed early. He must need his strength. It's been dark twenty minutes when you walk over their freshly cut lawn, and slip in the back door. During the exceptionally dim hours before sleep, the questions turn to sex. You hear a bath running and a kettle on the stove. You know what that means. You are a diehard fan.

A razor glides on skin. It's a question of perspective—the fluid gliding questions the linearity of time. Or when you're listening outside the door it does; you know what the shaving's for. You understand smooth skin above all. Paper invitations could not be as formal.

The box of spiders on the front seat of your car is half-empty. Daylight is the time to sell them. Now, with the imagined lather hinting to your ear pressed against the door's wood, you cannot think of a polite way to introduce your work.

Spider salesmen are misunderstood at night.

The sound of the old man's chair comes from another part of the house, as smooth as an electric razor. You take heed. You move away from it right past an open bedroom door.

It's too easy to keep ahead of this old clown. You're careful. You're not stupid, but why not have some fun, waiting for the woman to get her young body ready?

She opens the door in an explosion of steam and you retreat downstairs. He can't go there. It was too close.

You climb up the ladder on the side of an old dumbwaiter shaft and you can see into the bedroom.

The bed has moved up into the sitting position. She's lifted the old guy onto it. She pulls her nightgown over her head and lets it drop to the floor.

Her black hair is stringy from sweat. She's dark with no tan lines and the ridge of her spine curves like a slow whip. The old man's eyes are closed. She takes his right hand and cups a breast with it. As their breath quickens, she leans her head into his. Both faces are hidden by her dark wet hair. When she pulls her head back, she's holding his face in both hands, she's looking at him, impossible, impossible, and his eyes are open too.

The bed lowers with a low buzzing as she lies limp

on his paralyzed body. When it's flat she rolls over and smiles, then covers them both with a dark green sheet. He sighs.

"It just gets better," she says, lighting a cigarette and holding it to his lips. He laughs and then coughs.

"Doesn't it?" she asks quietly, taking a drag of her own.

"Of course it does," he says, closing his eyes.

"I wasn't sure. I didn't know if it would."

"How could you?"

"You knew," she says, holding the cigarette for him. "You knew exactly what would happen. You know exactly what will happen."

"There you go," he says, smiling.

"There you go."

"I know everything."

"Sometimes."

"Sometimes. Exactly." He wrinkles his nose.

"How can a person be so sure of himself?" she asks, scratching his nose. "There?"

"The side."

"There?"

"There."

She puts the cigarette in the ashtray on the bed table, and presses her palms to the sides of his face, rubbing his eyebrows, his cheeks, his neck. She bites his chin and laughs.

"Do you believe that man from this morning had spiders to sell?" she asks him, picking up the cigarette again.

"Yes."

"I don't. Who would buy them?"

"What do you think he was doing?"

"I don't know. I didn't like the way he looked at me."

"Can you make a small adjustment?"

"I just can't imagine why he would make up such a thing though," she says, reaching under the sheet.

"Thanks. He wouldn't."

They both lie on their backs, staring at the ceiling, and she yawns.

"I think a person might make something up if they were caught," she says. "But what did we catch him at?"

"Nothing," he says. "He was selling spiders. Some people use them to catch other bugs. I think I'll buy you some for your birthday, as a matter of fact. Make sure you take his card out of my pocket before that woman does the wash."

"It's not spiders I want, mister."

"Easy," he says. "I'm not the man I used to be."

She turns off the light and moves closer to him in the sudden darkness. It's not right. The mood is ruined. With the light off, your body forgets for a moment where you are. By heart, you descend, your legs waiting for solid ground.

It's still early enough to catch Rita. If it's a good day she'll be praying by the side of her bed with a slight smile. If it's bad, she'll have a look on her face as she turns out the light.

It will remind you of your mother crying at the kitchen table as you hurried to catch the school bus. It was as if she saw the future, saw her only son going door to door, though she could not guess why. She knew he could not step out of the dark. He would be misunderstood.

You see Rita sigh as she comes out of the shower. With a surprised look, she lets the towel drop and moves gracefully from room to room, naked with wet hair. Her house is lit by small lamps in corners and all the curtains are drawn. She carries her extra weight easily, and as she drinks a glass of water in the light of the fridge, she could be looking into your eyes, though she makes no sign she sees you.

You hope one day to move as lightly, to imagine yourself alone when you're not.

drowning

I watched the drowning man leave the pool. His heart still beat but it would be finished soon. His face was blue and he brushed past me, his cold skin infecting my cotton sundress with its dampness.

Jesus, what a job, I said, rubbing dried bubble gum from my lip.

What? he asked, sitting with his back against the side of the house.

You're drowning, right?

I'm on a break.

I knew that. I could see it. He sat shivering in the shade and lit a cigarette.

I know that, I said. You don't have to explain to me.

Of course not, he said, taking a drag on his cigarette.

I just said, what a job—that's all I said. I was commenting. I wasn't judging.

It sounded like you were judging.

I'm sorry.

We watched each other, me standing in sunlight, him shaking in the dark.

It's sunny, I said, why sit in the shade?

He laughed and shook his head.

What's so funny? I asked.

Everyone thinks they know my job. Why? Do I tell you how to do your job?

I guess . . .

I guess not. That's right. I'm doing my job the best I can and for God's sake, if I want to sit here and convulse from the cold, that's my right.

I'm sorry, I said.

What's your job? he asked.

To lose my mind and fade to nothing in a nursing home.

Wow, he said, smiling.

It's not glamourous, I know.

No. I'd rather do mine. Yours is tough.

Not really, I said, blushing.

I looked down at him and I was suddenly sure he could see up my dress. I felt my face burn hotter and sat down beside him. It was a relief to be out of the sun.

The shade is warmer, he said, now that you're here.

I held out my hand, two fingers splayed, to take his smoke, and he gave it to me. Our fingers touched and between the heat and the cold, it was something.

His Chevy Nova had been parked in the sun in front of the house all day. We fucked in the back seat.

I had never done that before, with the windows down, in broad daylight.

Stretching back on the sticky vinyl seat, I wiped sweat from my face and said he better get back to work. He was no longer blue.

I'm done, he said. My job is to pretend I'm drowning.

My job is to fuck delusional men, I said.

Across the street a little girl in cut-offs and no shirt sat on a dried lawn and watched us. We needed a moment.

Spit blue from candy shone on her chin. Her job was to watch adults fuck up the world around her.

A voice called and she nodded, then turned and ran into a house, her bare brown back disappearing through the door like a hamster going wild through a hole in the wall.

you still don't

We were digging holes in the ground and someone said wait, wait, wait. It was harder or easier as the day wore on and the sun lifted you, or beat you down, depending on your spirit, depending if you had the strength to imagine an evening after work, or if you went home to cold water and falling asleep to a ball game on the radio. That was how it worked.

But someone said wait, wait, wait and it was Ernie, back from the bush where four hundred metres away he had gone to take a dump and probably smoke a cigarette in the shade of the trees, where the air would be cool, but thick and stringy compared to the dust of the summer fallow.

And we looked at him, glad to be taken from the work, because the work wasn't important even though we talked about it all day long and at night every time we went for a beer. Did you see how that guy digs holes? He digs holes funny. We thought whoever wasn't with us must be queer and how did someone come to be with us?—a mystery, for sure. If I ever have a son, we'd say, he'll get a real job. But our fathers had told us time and again that real jobs were not for us, and also that this was a real job, and this would make us appreciate and it did, ten years down the road, running into someone from that summer. They'd say Jesus, I never had it so good, and we would laugh.

But Ernie told us to wait and he said come and see, but there were hundreds of men on that pipeline and we were only a small part, maybe six of us, and we said we have work to do and he knew that already. He was a hard worker, except when he left to sit in the shade and smoke when we were near some trees. He once walked half a mile there and half a mile back but he only did that once. He said it was too far, he said he knew when he was halfway there it was too far.

So he told us wait, stop what you're doing, we can all take a break and we didn't believe him. They said you can have lunch, they said it's required by law but the pipeline guys didn't see it that way and the money was good and we'd all have a couple weeks off at the end, before school or whatever it was that we did.

He told us come see what he saw, we said we can't and we can't. He kept talking and didn't pick up his shovel so we knew it wasn't over and we said what is it? And we wondered if it was only an exceptional shit and we didn't want to see that though we might be impressed, but he said no no no I'm serious and we wondered what to do.

In all the time before and all the time since I've seen many dead bodies on TV and in movies, but I never saw one for real and Ernie said it was a body he said it was a corpse and we asked him what kind? Fat or thin? Young or old? Woman or man? Though we all assumed it was a woman because these days men die in bed or in car accidents or with heart attacks in malls or old-timer hockey games. We all thought it was a woman but how was too much to bear.

He said he didn't know and we became quiet. What do you mean, you don't know? we asked and he was quiet too. Whether something had happened or not, it might as well have.

We have all this digging to do, we said. We have these holes to make and what do you mean you can't say? We all stopped for water and we all waited for Peter, who seemed like the leader sometimes. He lit a cigarette and we all drank water and the sun's work was far from our mind at the time. Our T-shirts were off but we kept them tucked into our pants—in case the inspector showed up. We weren't allowed a tan and out here in the middle of the prairie we were still supposed to wear hard hats and safety glasses. The hats were good against the sun, the glasses we'd lost long ago and there were only two weeks left on the job. We all talked big. Fuck you. Hire someone else to dig holes. But they never asked about the glasses anyway.

Peter asked Ernie what the hell he was talking about, was it a psychic vision? We laughed but still imagined bodies and evil. Ernie laughed too but it was plain to see he didn't want to.

He finally said it looked like a shallow grave and a shoe. What kind of shoe? A little girl's shoe, he said. You see, we thought, we were right. This is evil. There is evil here, or near here. We all knew women and we all knew girls.

This wasn't the old days, though it was close. The small towns we lived in while working, they were close. In the middle of nowhere, a community pasture or a field of canola, we might find a small wooden shack with a government plaque saying this site is a heritage site. This site is an original homestead and we knew with our shovels and the hard breaking of our bodies that someone had done something once, something harder than our lives, something lasting way past their own.

But the sun goes on like something biological, the sun beats on without words and cannot be argued with. We were afraid. We knew things about women and we all knew girls.

So we wanted to find the body and we wanted to make something right but this old town was new to us and we did not know the legends.

But that summer has turned into the old days and that summer we all had friends. I loved a girl called Stacey, but she was my best friend. The things she said, the secrets she told me, were too much. I wanted to tell her I am not a smart man. I wanted to tell her don't laugh at my jokes. There were things I wanted to say. Sometimes, she said, I want to talk to a man without fighting to keep his hands off me.

She was dumb and blind to my own hidden heart. I knew what it said, I knew it said want. I knew what it wanted.

This girl in the grave had us all thinking. How new is she? we said. I don't know, I don't know, we have to go dig. We have to dig right here we said but Peter's face was turning red and something was on his mind, he said we have to find whatever it is.

Wait, wait, wait, Ernie said. We can still do the work. We can still dig holes. I'll go and dig over there in the shade. We thought it was funny, not really, but it's easy to laugh. Fuck you, we said, you've been to that shade. We want the shade too.

That summer was the longest one ever. I smoked very little. I worked very hard. The sun existed, doing its work, and I did mine. I had no time for anything else. We dug and we dug, through hard ground and soft.

We saw what he meant when we got there. A little shoe, a little shoe of some colour too faded to see. And it looked like a grave, but what did we know except movies?

We talked to each other, but not about her, we thought we found clues. We spoke like scientists but we didn't know. The words we used did not approach our fear. We thought we found clues. Does this look like something, we'd ask? Is this a root or a bone? Every layer of dark decomposition turned into a rag of a skirt.

We dug harder, we worked harder. We all knew women but we didn't speak of them. We said this has to be something but quickly the original plot of the grave was gone and who knew how to read what had been there before our hard work?

We stopped digging and took some water and Peter said too late, we've got to get going and we looked at the sun and knew it was time so we ran back to where we were supposed to be, all except Peter and Ernie. When we saw they weren't running we walked too.

In camp they thought we were smoking up in the bush. They thought we were slacking off. By the time we get the results the job will be over, they said, so we can't even test you, but it can't happen again. We said okay.

Some of the others thought we were heroes. We never told them we were looking for a little girl's body. We never said a thing. How does a man become a hero for smoking drugs in the shade while others work in the sun?

I shared a room with Ernie. I didn't sleep well. We didn't really talk. He said once I'm glad we didn't find a body. I guess there wasn't one, he said, by way of apology. You didn't know, I said. You still don't.

We had to work Sunday to make it up. Stacey called and said where were you? I told her they thought we were smoking dope in the trees. She said but you wouldn't do that. I said well, we didn't do all we should have is all. She said well I know you did all you could. They just don't know you.

I said I couldn't sleep last night and I was up at six, digging in the field. When she didn't speak I said these days I'm tired and if I want to sit in the shade and smoke that's just what I'll do.

She said I don't know what you're talking about. We left it at that.

the saint

The saint's drumming by you in his ordinary car. You're stuck on the corner with new socks, a clean shirt, and bright-coloured money.

You've spent all your time, your whole life and the meantime, walking between one driveway and the next on your right.

You've got a drink of biblical size that hasn't been stirred in ages but the first house you went to is ancient and large and the man at the door baffled you and the Lord, as his wife stood in the corner wrapped in Saran Wrap and winking and singing come get me you make-believe bastard.

And when did you become a story? When did you become fiction? When did you become less than the man at the door who just baffled the Lord? And how is it his wife, she sees you right now but when her hunger is passed you're as thick as the air? You might as well be part of her little dream though it hurts to imagine that you're really here, or not really here.

You caused the whole scene or she did or he did and now with all the ice melting, with the whole world warming, that means drinks getting watered and you can't handle that so you switch to red wine and drink it just warm or steaming and sleep on the lawn if it takes you to morning.

You hear names upon names upon names but they mean only colours which means you hear it with your eyes and I'm sorry you say and you mean it.

The saint's walking round with his mystical pipe or his fancy long bong and he's blessing us all from the bottom on up.

Start tomorrow, he says, and lists reasons and reasons and the good and the order to do it but then falls asleep with small towns on his lips.

Listen, I've never heard a prophet say Asquith or Perdue, not even Saskatoon, and where are we from if we're not from the city, the homeland or the cradle of civilization?

But this man is unorganized and let it slip as he slept and he's a saint but he knows me and he showered at my house and I'm sorry, I'll miss him but I'm off to work and that's enough. That's enough; he's all sick and scabby and I think he's got worms and the city I live in is far from the journey the texts shouted out—we've got meat and potatoes and I hope to hell he's gone in the morning.

I'm off at the bus stop and there he is naked in winter in his iced-over car wearing a blanket from my bed and smiling and shivering, drumming the dash at the red light and I want it back, my blanket, but I don't need it really and the dumb-ass, he should have stolen my shirts and my pants.

He'll have a terrible time in a town like Asquith when he stops to get gas.

a grey pattern of green

"The ladies and I have an understanding," the old man said. He licked his lips and winked.

"Which ladies, Mr. Anderson?"

The old man stared at James. His lower lip jutted out and his cheeks sunk in like he was sucking on something. He dabbed his left eye with a cloth napkin. It was leaky. His mouth and his eyes seemed like wounds, James thought, and it was because his body was so dry, like carved sticks.

Anderson reached across the table and gripped James' wrist.

"Take your pick, young man. These women you see all around."

James looked around the room. There were old women at every table. They were picking at food and dabbing their mouths with napkins.

"Where's your mother, James?" the old man asked, raising a glass of water to his lips.

"I thought she would be here by now," James said.

"Me too. Where are you going today?"

"Just back to the farm. She likes it there."

"I never heard her talk about the farm."

"Well, she likes it there. She's sad when we bring her back."

"Well."

"There's nothing else to do."

"Fair enough. She don't seem that sad when she's here."

James smiled. "She's not one of the ladies with the understanding is she?"

"I'm not tellin' you, you little bugger," Anderson chuckled. "We're all grown-ups here."

James looked around the room, smiling. Some of the old people were sad and some were angry. Anderson always seemed happy. James liked him because he always made up new stories. The others, when they talked to James, told him the same thing every time.

"Where the hell is she?" James asked.

"Don't know," he said. "Listen, I'm tired. Why don't you go get me a cup of coffee?"

"Okay, but if my mother—"

"Cripes James just go. You're makin' me sick whining about your mommy. One of them bastards with the white coats stole my cane, I think. Alright. Soon as you get that damn coffee I'm gonna have to take you on with my bare hands."

James went and got the coffee. The old man really did look tired.

"Thanks," he said. "Now go get that umbrella over there so I can give you a beating."

"You know them bastards with the white coats listen to me, Mr. Anderson," James said. "I can get them to dope you up real good."

"You're right. Sorry James, I'll be nice. I should've

known you're on their side."

"That's right."

"Then you know what them stupid college boys made me do last night."

"Well, they don't tell me everything," James admitted. "Like why would I be sitting here waiting for my mother if I knew *everything?*"

"I told you: quit whining. She'll be here when she feels like it. Now I'll tell ya what those kids made me do."

"I don't remember asking you to tell me."

"I'm telling you," the old man said. "Look around the room and tell me if you see anything different."

James looked around the room. It was the same as it ever was: plain brown tables; black chairs; the same faded drapes that hung in bunches all along the wall that was glass; the dull green and off-white pattern on yellowing wallpaper; the bulletin board with the bingos and classes and movies listed for the coming week.

"I don't see anything."

"The wallpaper, James," the old man said, looking around at the walls. "Not these bastards working now, but the night people."

"Yeah."

"I had an appointment, you know. But those bastards, those young ones, they're lazy. You know what I mean James?"

"Yeah. They're lazy."

"Right, and they're fat. Anyway, that's why I'm tired. They come to my room and say they're on to me, James. We know what's going on Anderson, they say."

"Did they really know?"

"Can I take the risk?"

"I guess not."

"So they say they know, so I say what and I play real dumb right, so's not to incriminate myself. I play it real cool. They already took my cane James, like I said."

"Right."

"So they say we got work for you, they say, or the jig's up."

"The jig's up?"

"That's what they say, James. The jig's up, they say."

"So what did you do?"

"I went with them. What could I do?"

"Nothing—the jig would be up."

"That's what they said, so I went with them."

The old man dabbed his eye with his napkin. He coughed, took a drink of coffee and licked his lips. His tongue looked dry like a lizard, but his mouth was wet. It looked fake, like a sudden movement could smear it right to his ears.

"I'm getting too old James. Those buggers are killing me. I'm not so old as the rest of 'em, but I'm old."

"So where'd they take you?"

"Here. Those fat kids sat right here, at this table. They had a bottle of whiskey and they sat at this table and drank."

"That's not so bad."

"They drank and they made me repaper this room. It was their job. So they sat and played cards and drank while I did their work."

"But you had an appointment."

"That's right James, but what could I do? They said they knew everything."

"Maybe you should cut back on some of your dealings, lay low for a while—just till the heat's off."

"I'm not that old. I gotta use my brain," he said, tapping the side of his head. "Gotta keep sharp so I don't get old."

The old man laughed and his whole thin body shook. "Besides, all those women, they like the way I treat them when I've got money."

"I guess you're right," James said, looking around the room at all the walls.

"It's the same damn pattern James," the old man said, shaking his head. "You can't even tell."

He sighed and rubbed his eyes.

James looked around the room. He watched the entrance to the dining room hoping to see his mother, and listened to the old man, who was telling another story. This one was about James' mother. The old man said they knew each other when they both were young. He said he worked one summer for the railroad and they were in James' hometown for a few weeks and he met her when she worked at the grocery store.

James tried to imagine the old man as young. For years he had tried to imagine his mother as young.

Once, she had told him a story a few years ago when she was going through her things, getting ready to move into the home. It was her idea. She said she couldn't remember things anymore. Then, in an old box, she found a small silver cross.

Years earlier she had given it to her boyfriend. But one day she found it on the dirt path he took to school every day. The path went through a field, then under the trees in the vacant lot by her house. She had stayed by her bedroom window, watching the path. She held the cross and sometimes cried, she told James, because she would never have lost anything he had given her, if he'd given her anything. He never came looking for it, and he never mentioned he'd lost it.

His mother had sat there, deliberate in every way, as old people are, even when they're not moving. She'd said she was dumb in those days, when she was young. It was just a little thing, but she had cried sometimes at night because of it, and her love had turned to hate. She cried when she told James, even though she was old, and he held her and listened.

He was afraid he would hurt her, then. He had never thought of her as old until she had started to cry and he had held her and she was small. Then he tried to imagine her young, and he hated that boy who had lost the cross.

"He wasn't your father James," she had said that day, looking at him with wet eyes. She had never told him who his father was and he had stopped asking.

He had cleared his throat and she had watched him, scared, ready for the old fight about his father. But he wasn't going to say anything about that. He just hugged her and tried to imagine her young. They were nervous about whatever the other might say. He felt his mother's hand on his shoulder and looked up to see her smiling down at him.

"What did this old man tell you today, Jimmy?" she asked.

"I didn't tell him a thing, Jenny," the old man said. James thought he looked embarrassed.

"What took you so long, Mom? Everyone's waiting out at the farm. Kim's there with her new little boy. She wanted to come but I told her to stay. She's exhausted; he's just a week old."

"It's okay. We'll go see her, eh?" she said, putting her hand on the old man's shoulder. He coughed and dabbed his left eye.

They said goodbye to Mr. Anderson and walked out to the car.

When they got to the edge of town, his mother smiled and looked at James.

"Go the old way again," she said, "and tell me who used to live where."

So they went the old way and James told her as much as he knew and she smiled and nodded or shook her head and frowned, depending on where they drove by, and who had lived there.

their names

He started rubbing materials together. Notions filled his head. She said very little, but he knew she meant it; it was time for him to go.

But the world was too large. There was trouble out there. He knew it. It was the people; the people were the trouble. He did his job. He took care of himself—eating solids and drinking liquids.

It made him sick, the things people do.

"Aren't you gone yet?" she asked. She had just come in from outside and she was combing her hair.

"Exactly where should I go?" he asked, putting the materials on the table.

"Not my problem."

"What?"

"I said NOT-MY-PROB-LEM."

He tried to make his mind think of rude gestures but could not. He could think of nothing. She used to sing him songs. She wasn't always one of the people.

"You're lying," he said.

"What are you talking about?"

"You're lying," he said again.

"See," she said. "You have no idea. I'm doing something wrong, so you say I'm lying."

"Well, you said it's wrong."

"Okay. It's not wrong. But you think it's wrong and so you say I'm lying."

He stared at her.

"There are many things you can say, any number, like—"

"A variety," he said.

"—like I'm an idiot, like I'm a slut—"

"You're none of those things," he said, looking down at the materials on the table.

She saw he could say no more and stood looking at him. He was capable of huge naked blocks of feeling, almost none of which could be fit into the shape of words. It was one of the things she had loved about him, in the beginning.

"What are you thinking?" she asked him.

"Nothing," he said.

He kept staring at the materials on the table. What can you possibly do with materials such as these? he thought. They will make nothing. You might rub them together but eventually they will wear to nothing.

"Of course you're thinking something," she said, walking toward him.

"You never used to ask me so many questions. You used to make me feel like I didn't need to speak and now everything I say is wrong."

"That's not true," she said.

He looked up from the table and they said nothing and watched each other.

"I was thinking about these materials," he said.

When she smiled he thought she might let him stay. His whole body beat like a heart and he smiled back. There was heat in the skin of his face.

When she laughed his face burned.

"Those 'materials' are called something," she yelled, shaking her head. "Those are two sharpening stones. They're for knives. They sharpen the knives."

"I didn't know the word."

"You don't know any of the words. We speak but—"

"I know I can't build anything with these . . . MATERIALS!" he said, jutting his chin out in a challenge.

"No kidding."

"Well, then . . ." a tear grew in the corner of his right eye. He watched her and wondered why he didn't know the things she wanted him to know. He loved her, he knew that. She didn't love him anymore, he knew that.

"Well, then . . ."

"You said that."

"Well, then," he said, walking toward the door, "I don't need those . . ."

She watched him and smiled an I-told-you-so smile.

" . . . THINGS!"

"Sharpening stones," she said, laughing.

He took one more look around the house and he knew what things were for. He knew the use of most items. He didn't need her anymore. He had to leave before he destroyed something.

He heard her laughing as he walked down the walk. Her laughter turned to tears behind him and he looked at the ugly world around him: people buying things; people riding things; people running into one another all the time.

He didn't need those things. Why did he need their names?

the sorts of things a man should know

When his blind father died, there was a hitch in his breath as he crossed the street to buy flowers. He imagined it. The flowers were real.

Soon after the death of his father, his mother called him on the phone. Your poor father's dead, she said. How do you know? Well, it wouldn't surprise me, she said.

The day after his blind father died, he didn't open the store. He took the day off. He didn't make a tearful speech in his mind. He didn't say he would have wanted it this way.

His father went to heaven, I guess. That's the thing about blind people: they all go to heaven. They're good just living, what with no seeing and all. They're good just putting up with it.

When his blind father died, he thought of marbles and stones. What would his father wear? He always wore sunglasses and no glass eyes, ever. Just empty sockets, looking rubbed and raw behind his shades.

The day after his father died, his mother came up from Georgia. Why was she there? Just to come up from Georgia, he thought. Just to come north to the small town from somewhere down south. She brought her new husband and he wasn't nearly as southern as she despite having grown up there. She was from Perdue, Saskatchewan.

With his father's death, the end began. He didn't want the store. He had no interest in Braille books. The market didn't grow. It was the only store in town and the blind people all knew of it. What else was there to do but go on the way it was? He explained it to his son, who was seven. Grandpa's dead, he said. Oh, said the boy, is he gone? Yes, he's gone forever. Oh, said the boy.

When his blind father died, he went through the closet looking for clothes. They'd been the same size since he was twenty-one. He found a soft brown suit of his father's and wore it to the store the next day.

The morning his father died, he looked in the mirror. You're an ugly bastard, he said, just like your father.

When his father died, there were no more tricks, no more jokes. How did his father ever know the length of the cigar he was lighting? He used to label his father's CDs wrongly on purpose. What good would that do now?

The day after his father died, he asked his mother to stay

at his home while she was there for the funeral. She wanted to stay at his father's house. His father being dead, he said no. It was never your house.

When his blind father died, he went to Graceland. His father had gone right after the divorce. I should have gone there to be married, he said. What they say about blind people hearing and smelling more, he said, it might be true. I smell pretty good. But I wanted to see Graceland. That's the only time I really wanted to see, he said, when your mother left and I went to Graceland. He went to Elvis' house when his father died and looked carefully, wondering what it was his father had wanted to see.

Weeks after his father died, he began to get insurance money. His father had spent most of his money in life on insurance. Someday I'll die, he said. It only makes sense—I'm blind.

Soon after his father died, he saw his mother cry. She was beautiful and his father had been ugly. She had loved him because he could not love her face. He never worried she would leave him because he was ugly. He didn't know how ugly he was. In the end she couldn't believe someone could love her without using his eyes.

When his blind father died, there was little to say: a man dead, his son wondering the sorts of things a man should know.

He crossed the street to buy flowers on the average

overcast day. He waited in the doorway of the shop for a bus to pull away so he could cross back. The cheap bouquet in his hand would last and last, the woman had told him. The pale flowers shamed him.

What kind of flowers are you looking for? she had asked.

I don't know, he said.

She ushered him into the cool display area and left him behind the glass with all the flowers while she took another customer. He looked in bewilderment at the shapes and colours around him, knowing at their ends all the stems were wet and cold. He tried to see all the flowers.

She came back and saw that he was helpless.

These will last a very long time, she said, handing him a bunch of soft-coloured flowers.

He nodded and smiled.

That's a beautiful suit, she said, her hand on his shoulder, gently guiding him to the door, back to where it was warm.

no hands for taking

John pulled the truck into McDonald's and went too quickly through the parking lot to the end. He always took two spots, at least; partly the big truck, partly he didn't care.

"So where's the woman?" I asked, after we were sitting down eating our food. He didn't know who I meant. I told him the one at the house, the one whose yard we just cleaned, the old one he said shouldn't give the house to her son who would ruin it.

"Why?"

"I just need the money," I said. "Why couldn't she just pay us?"

"She's not there. I told you. She's in Ontario, visiting her son."

It didn't take us long to eat, but I almost fell asleep. John was reading the paper and I was watching the kids play.

I saw a boy, about six maybe, who wanted to play and run like the others but couldn't, or was afraid, or something. He watched the kids in the play area like they were on television. He ate his hamburger slowly, and swung his legs over the plastic edge of his chair. He sucked pop through a straw and then he was done.

He gathered the garbage in a paper bag and took it to the trash can right by the playground. The children screamed and laughed, sliding into a bin of coloured balls.

I dozed off watching the kid, trying to imagine his thoughts. When John woke me up, I was startled. The boy was back with his mother, embarrassed and sucking on an asthma inhaler.

We stood up and left to take the junk from the old woman's yard to the dump.

At the end of the day, everyone at the shop went for a beer. Everyone but me and John's dad, who owned the company. I took a bus home; he stayed, working underneath a gravel truck.

I had no food so I stopped at the convenience store under my apartment to buy eggs, butter and cigarettes. I hadn't meant to keep the apartment for so long. It was nice enough, but small. There was no bedroom and the bathroom was right off the kitchen.

I switched on the TV and went into the kitchen to put on a pot of water. Then I put the eggs and butter into the fridge.

Sitting on the couch I emptied my pockets and found a key folded in a five-dollar bill. I held it in my left hand and smoked a cigarette.

I thought about the old lady who lived in that house, and her son who was no good and might get the house. It sounded like he didn't deserve anything good, and I wondered why.

I wished I had left the key in the mailbox, like I'd meant to, after finding it in a cinder block near the back door. I had thought about it too much. What's in that house? I thought, and if the old lady's so old she's going to give it to her son, would she miss anything anyway?

The water boiled and I put some eggs in there. I was going to boil them for sandwiches, even though I knew John would stop at a burger place every day.

I ate a couple eggs and fell asleep watching a baseball game.

John called the next morning and said there was no work. He said he'd call when there was.

My little apartment smelled like it always did and I couldn't fall back asleep so I sat up and lit a cigarette.

The TV was still on so I turned it off, then called my mother to borrow her car.

She came and picked me up and I drove us to a restaurant where she bought us toast and coffee. She told me all about a movie last night but I didn't really listen. I wanted to, and I meant to, but I was trying to think of a job I might like.

My mind wandered. I saw the waitress and I thought she was nice. Her shoes were beaten up, but why buy new shoes when you just use them to walk on? Her uniform was old and frayed at the collar a bit, but clean.

She looked happy but there were fine lines on her face that seemed too old for her. Nancy, her name tag said.

When I wasn't looking at the waitress I was thinking

of a job I might like, but I had no idea. I wanted a job I could stay clean in, I thought. I wanted to dress nicely in the morning and stay sharp and crisp all day, then come home and relax in the jeans I wore to work now.

But my mother was looking at me with a slightly pained smile.

"You know, after everything, I miss your father."

"I know that, Mom."

"We never knew all we had."

"I know."

She smiled again. "You can't know. But you will. It comes with getting old."

"I think you're right, Mom. But I know a few things."

"I know. I know," she said, brightening a little, putting on a nicer smile. "Now, what kind of job are you going to do?"

"I'm trying to think but I don't really know."

"Darlene's girl, Patty, she just got a new job. She reads newspapers all day and she loves it."

She took a sip of coffee and looked at me.

"You know, one of those things, I forget what they're called—she reads the papers and cuts out articles and mails them to someone."

"Yeah, I know what you mean."

"And she likes it. She really likes it."

"Yeah, but she's in Toronto."

"No," she said, raising her eyebrows and leaning toward me across the table. "She moved back. She's living with Darlene. I think it was when Mike left. I never liked him."

"Me neither," I said, watching her shake her head. Her eyes were getting wet and she wore her weak, sorrowful smile again.

"I can't fathom God's plan," she said. "But Darlene's been so sad. Then a few weeks ago she called me and said Patty's coming home."

My mother looked out the window, to where the dry sun of the morning worked at burning the asphalt. The parking lot was full of ten-year-old cars and faded cigarette packs leaned against curbs waiting for wind or rain to move them.

"I said praise the Lord, but I wondered why Patty would be coming home."

I dropped my Mom at her house and when she asked I told her I'd stay for supper when I brought back her car.

I went to a donut shop with the paper and sat there smoking with the want ads, a coffee and a glass of water.

There was an ad for night work at a warehouse. I thought it would be perfect, then I saw the address; I'd applied there three times in the last few months. I got an interview the first time. I don't know what I did wrong.

It was almost too much. You do what you can. I spent every working day looking for work, when I wasn't working. It never amounted to anything. You tell yourself keep trying but in the mirror you're looking for a hump or a growth or some other big ugly sign telling the world how small you are.

And it wouldn't be bad if that were the extent of it. It wouldn't be bad if you didn't see people getting everything so easily. It wouldn't be bad if there were one day where you walked into everyone's houses and you took all their things and put them all in a pool.

"Here," you would say, to the people like them and the people like you—to everyone—"Here. Start over. Let's make it fair. This time it's fair."

I stubbed out my cigarette and walked over to the pay phone.

"Benson's Contracting, John speaking."

"Hi, it's Ed. Listen, I'm just wondering if you can find me something around the shop tomorrow if there's nothing else."

"I don't know, man. You know. That's my dad's call, really."

I didn't say anything.

"You know. I'll talk to him—" he put his hand over the phone and I heard muffled voices for a couple of minutes.

" . . . I doubt it," he said, to someone.

Then he came back to me: "Listen, he says did you find a key at that old lady's house yesterday?"

"No," I said, and my heart sped up as I said it.

"I didn't think so," he said. "I already told him—"

There was noise on the line, then John's father came on.

"Listen," Mr. Benson said. "I was just talking to Mrs. Ward. She said she had a key in the backyard, hidden, for her son, and forgot about it. I said I'd ask if you found it but it's probably in the dump by now."

"Pardon?"

"Yeah, she said she had a house key hidden there, you know, for her son or neighbours or something I guess, but I told her—"

"Oh, a key in the backyard we cleaned yesterday?"

"What other yard?" he said loudly. "Yes, that yard. Anyway, I told her . . ."

He started coughing on the other end.

"Listen," he said, "it's a waste of time. I'll tell her no."

"No," I said, "I did find it. I couldn't hear you right, I guess. I wasn't thinking. It must be too loud in here."

I looked around the donut store. There were two customers. One old man sat in the corner, doing a crossword puzzle with his face five inches from the paper on the table. The other one was about fifty, maybe a salesman. He was watching me and chewing as I spoke. He smiled and nodded and I blushed, then he looked out the window.

"Listen," I said, "I've got it right here. I can just take it to her. I'm right by there now."

"Well, no. It doesn't matter. She's out of town, I don't know why she cares—you know, make another one. Have one cut but—"

"No, I'll just go leave it in her mailbox."

"It's no big deal, really, but if you want to—"

"Well, I'm just saying, I meant to, so I might as well, if I'm right here, I mean I meant to leave it in her mailbox when we were done there."

"Yeah, okay," he said. "That would be great."

"Okay, no problem," I said. "Now about—"

"Uh, wait. Listen. She's out of town right now, okay, so why don't you take her mail in. You know. They say to do it."

"What? Go into her house? Oh, and just leave—"

"Yeah, just leave the key by her front door, with the mail."

"Alright."

"Okay," he said. "Thanks."

"Yeah, no problem," I said. "But what about work tomorrow?"

"No. We got nothing tomorrow."

"Well maybe there—"

"No, maybe Monday. Come get your cheque on Friday if you want," he said, and then hung up.

I applied at the warehouse again. I applied at some other places too, then I went home to sleep.

My mother answered the door smiling.

"Hi Ed," she said, and hugged me like we hadn't seen each other for years. Then she took my baseball cap off and put it on the shelf by the door.

"Why?" I asked, brushing my hand over my hair. My head was itchy. I took off my shoes then reached for my cap. She brushed lint off my shoulders and shook her head at me.

"You look so good without a hat on," she whispered.

Then I heard Darlene in the kitchen.

"No!" I heard her say. "Well, I'll come right over! No, we have to get it sorted out, Mavis."

"Oh," my mother said, "Darlene and her girl

stopped by for dinner."

I felt myself blushing and she put a hand on my back and moved me toward the kitchen.

Darlene waved as we came into the kitchen. She was holding the phone to her ear and beaming at us as we walked through the door.

Patty sat at the table looking down at the cup of coffee in front of her. Her eyes were in the shadow of the dark hair that framed her face. When she looked up with a small smile, her brown eyes shone suddenly.

"Hi Patty," I said.

Then my mother did her work: pushing me into the chair across from Patty; telling us both what the other liked; filling Patty's mug and getting me one of my own.

"Well, we better get going," Darlene said, hanging up the phone.

"What!?" my mother said, a bit loudly.

Their acting was absurd; they finished each other's sentences and repeated cues to each other, and both through smiles too happy for the news they were telling.

Apparently, a friend had fallen and broken her wrist. They had to go and help build something after they took this friend to the hospital. It had something to do with a charity, or some volunteer organization I had never heard of.

"We could be very late," my mother said as they left. "I'll go with Darlene so you give Patty a ride home will you dear?"

"Of course," I said.

Patty and I hadn't seen each other for years. I didn't know what to tell her, really, so we ate the food my mother had prepared and talked about movies and TV shows. After a while, we relaxed and it turned into a nice evening.

She told me about a small town in Ontario that existed only as a name, really. It was long ago hidden between two larger towns, the borders of which were unclear or non-existent.

"The old people who had lived there still know who they are," she said. "I mean, they know the others from the town, and their children. But the young people don't know."

"That's sad," I said, chuckling.

She laughed too.

"No, I mean it," I said. "It is a little sad."

"Well, I don't know. In a way it's perfect—they both get what they need. The young ones are at home in the larger community and the old ones still live in it the way it used to be. Neither is hurt; both pity each other, but both survive."

"I guess that's true," I said, and got up to take her plate. "I think you're right. Too bad a couple larger cities wouldn't swallow this one up."

She laughed.

"I know what you mean," she said. "But I think I really like Saskatoon. I couldn't wait to leave when I was younger. But I'm glad to be back. I guess that's just what happens.

"You never know," she added, shrugging.

I didn't know what to say next. I stood by the sink

and watched her. She was a pretty woman. Her dark eyes seemed so much stronger than when I had known her before.

I thought I should ask if she wanted a drink, but I knew my mother wouldn't have any in the house.

We looked at each other. She looked happy.

"Well," I said, and then I got tense, like I always do.

"Oh," she said, blushing a little. "I guess we should go then. You have work tomorrow."

"Okay," I said, as she stood up.

I wanted to tell her why I hadn't left this town. I wanted her to think there were good reasons. I wanted to find the words to tell her why I didn't know what to say to a girl like her. I wanted her to know it wasn't my fault.

When we knew each other before I had always been dumb; she would talk to me, because our parents were friends, and I couldn't look her in the eyes. Her thin beauty astonished me and I'd just smile weakly. My friends made crude comments when she left. She's nice to me, I would say. She's a nice girl.

Then they all left too. It's a dying town.

I don't know what she knew about me, but I wanted to tell her she shouldn't have come home. I wanted her to know that whatever hockey player she'd loved had been wrong to let her go.

"You haven't changed," was all I said.

"Neither have you," she said.

We got our things, turned out the lights and walked to the door.

"I'm sorry," I told her as soon as the front door closed behind us.

"For what?"

"You know," I said, smiling and pointing behind me with my thumb. "My mother, I guess. Your mother, too."

She didn't say anything and I opened the passenger door and she got in. I walked around the car and got in my side. We both rolled our windows down.

"There aren't even any bugs," she said.

"Yeah. Nice."

"Can I have a cigarette?" she asked.

I told her sure and got one for each of us. I was surprised that she smoked and I told her so. She said a lot changes, a lot can happen, as I pulled the car away from the curb.

"I know," I said. "That's true."

The street was almost deserted. It was dark in the way a city might get dark, almost light in some places, because of the buildings and the streetlights—yet seeming darker than a country road because of the stillness, the light where everything is but nothing moves. Too many night shifts had made me love this time.

"Anyway, like I say, I'm sorry about my mother," I said.

"I still don't know why," she said.

"Well," I said, feeling my face get red, "I think maybe she was, um, I think your mom and my mom were . . ."

"Trying to set us up?"

"Yeah," I said, nodding my head and relaxing a little.

"Yeah. Okay, it wasn't just me."

"No."

I drove slowly, not knowing what to say. When I looked over she was leaning on her door, with her face to the night air. We were both as young as we would ever be and I wanted the drive to last.

I told her about the key. I said I had to take it back that night and it would just take a minute. It was on the way.

We drove in silence for a few blocks. I stole glances at her when I could, looking at her in the dash-lights, and I remembered what all the boys had loved in school: the smile so ready, always at the corners of her mouth. It was that or her eyes, always a little too open, somehow; without the threatened smile, they might seem cartoonish, but with it, they seemed part of a girl so open that she would never say no, if a boy just had the nerve.

When we stopped in front of the old lady's house, Patty said she had to use the washroom. She walked up the sidewalk ahead of me and stood on the step while I unlocked the door.

"Oh, wait," she said. "I better finish my cigarette. She'll smell the smoke."

She sat on the step and motioned me to sit beside her. I did, and lit one of my own.

The street looked lush and green even in the sickly yellow of the streetlights. It was quiet. Some windows on the block were lit, some were not. I looked at her and she was watching me.

"You're nervous," she said.

"No," I said, laughing a little. Then I sighed to calm myself.

"It's okay. You're nervous because this isn't your house. That's good, I think."

"No. I'm scared of nothing sometimes, really."

"Well, I guess we shouldn't just hang around here, like it's a lounge or something," she said, standing up.

I stood up too and we took the mail in and laid it with the key on the floor by the door. Patty stood by the door. "I'll just wait here then, if you want to use the washroom," I said.

"No. I can wait. We should go," she said.

"No really, go ahead," I said, putting my hand on her shoulder. "I sometimes seem nervous, you know, it's stupid."

When she left to the bathroom I ran into the bedroom. I looked quickly through drawers. I wondered if she had a den, where was her desk? I thought I was quiet. I heard blood in my ears but none of my movements.

I couldn't find any money and I didn't know what else to look for. I ran to the door and was looking at pictures on the wall before she left the bathroom.

I heard Patty walk up behind me. I wasn't startled by her hand on my shoulder.

"I was just looking at these pictures," I said. "I guess you can see that though."

"Yeah," she said. "I know why you're nervous."

"What?" I asked, turning to face her.

"It's pretty obvious," she said, smiling.

"Well, we should get out of here."

I closed the door once she'd stepped out of the house and then passed her in my hurry to get to the car.

She was quiet the rest of the way. I thought she was embarrassed. I thought she was mad at me.

"I'm sorry," I said.

"What for?" she said, and that stumped me. What for?

"I don't think it's a good idea," she said. "I mean, I think you're a nice guy and, you know, but . . ."

"You're not looking for a relationship?" I asked, suddenly understanding.

"Exactly," she said. "Okay?"

"Sure."

"But we can—"

"Listen. We'll see each other now and then, though. It's good to see you. People leave and you never see them again."

I parked in front of her mother's house and we saw someone peek from the corner of the living room window.

"Well, I have to be up at four," she said.

"Oh, well, I guess this is it then. I don't have to be up that early, but . . ."

"What do you do?" she said.

"Nothing, really," I said. "I mean I'm looking for something better."

"I am too," she said.

Call me, she said. I said I would, and watched her walk up the walk to her mother's house. When the door shut after her I started the car.

Her window was still down and the green smell of the city in summer blew through the car as I turned off McKercher and onto Eighth Street.

Sitting at the next red light, there was no one else on the road, and I leaned my head back on the headrest. I lit a cigarette and sighed. Where's the money in that house, I thought. I mean besides stereos, besides appliances? Where's the money a guy could slip in his pocket? I waited through two more reds, alone at the intersection. Next time it turned green I drove through, and drove home.

there is a way

He took a pail in each hand and went into the house. He poured the paint, and was about to put the roller in.

"Is this the right colour?" he asked.

She didn't look up. She was looking through books in a cardboard box near the door to the kitchen.

"It's the paint I bought," she said. "I only bought one colour."

"Green," he said.

"I'm forgetting something. I know I am."

He rolled the roller in the tray and watched it swell with paint. It was green, alright.

"I don't think I've got everything in here," she said. She's been looking at the books off and on all morning.

"I sort of like the colour it is now," he said, turning to face her. She was on her knees, looking in the box. The paint dripped from the roller to the paper on the floor.

He remembered the first time she'd come home with her hair cut like that. It was summer and her skin was dark. There was a band of pale skin on the back of her neck. She was a beautiful woman, alright. He knew that.

Now it was summer again, and her whole neck was dark.

It was summer, and hot. Spring had been short and summer was long. There was no wind and it seemed the sun was the centre of the whole prairie sky, all day. There was a watering ban in Saskatoon, but he saw the back-yards of his neighbours over the fence. They were fresh and green.

She turned and looked at him, and he remembered the roller in his hand.

"Where should I start?" he asked.

"Anywhere," she said, looking puzzled. "Is this yours?" she asked, holding up a book.

He glanced quickly toward her, shrugged, and rolled a fat green line on the white wall.

"What?" she asked.

"Probably yours, I said."

"No."

"Maybe," he said, painting more quickly.

"I don't think so," she said.

He watched the roller leave dull green marks thick on the white. It was fuzzy at the edges, but still stood out clear against the old wall. It was green, alright, but he thought he might have gotten used to it.

"I don't want to miss any of your stuff," she said. He wasn't looking. He was painting the wall with his back to her. It made him feel good, now.

"It's okay," he said. "It's bound to happen"

"I think this book is yours."

"I don't know. If you're not sure, just keep it."

"I told you that colour was nice," she said, standing.

"I don't like it."

"Well, I guess it's that colour now."

"I guess so."

He turned to wet the roller in the tray again. He saw her staring at him. She was hurt, alright. Her eyes were wet.

"I don't know why you won't help me remember whose books these are," she said.

"I don't care."

"I'm just trying to do this right."

"I'm trying to paint this goddamn room," he said. "Why the hell am I trying to paint this goddamn room? I don't know. But I am."

"You promised," she said.

"And that's what I'm doing."

He bent down, wet the roller and turned to paint the wall.

"This one, for instance . . ."

"I don't care whose book it is. Don't ask me another goddamn book question. If you don't know, you keep the fucking book. I've forgotten it already, so just keep the book!"

"I don't want to keep it if it's yours," she said.

He kept painting. He started using the small brush. He got on the stool and stood painting by the ceiling. He didn't know how to paint, really, he didn't know the order, but he was bored with the roller.

He watched her leave the room and heard her turn the water on in the kitchen sink. She came back with her face tight and the edges wet.

"I'm going out for a cigarette," she said. "You gonna come?"

This is tough, alright, he thought, but somehow people do it. A cigarette couldn't hurt.

So he went outside and took the cigarette she gave him. His hands were all paint, so she lit it for him. It was a hot day, but they sat in the shade.

they're for you

He stood there drunk, half in the pool and half out of it. The pulse of water was still in his ears.

"What?" he asked.

The silhouette of a woman stood on the deck, outlined by the light coming from the house.

"What are you doing?" the shadow asked.

"Swimming."

"What are you doing here?"

It was his wife.

The water was warm and his upper body shivered. He could still feel the water in his head. He wanted to be underwater.

"I mean, you're not in Ireland."

"Obviously."

"Why are you here?"

"What about you?" he asked, his body shaking.

"I told you I wasn't going. You were still supposed to go."

His mind was slow from liquor and he was losing interest. He thought he might sleep in the water tonight.

"You never told me—you left a note."

"It doesn't matter."

He thought he saw a shadow on the edge of the

light. He was getting colder.

"You have to leave."

"What?" he said, stepping out of the pool.

"You better go."

"It's my house," he said, shaking and looking on the ground for his clothes.

"You're not supposed to be here."

"Where are my clothes?"

They stood and stared at each other.

"I've got to get a towel."

"Get away from me!" she screamed. He was sure there was another shadow behind her, the shadow of a man. But he could hardly see through the light.

He walked to his car and got in. He turned on the heater and watched more lights go on in the house. Staring at blurred dash-lights, he listened to the ocean in his ears. It pulled against the heartbeat in his wet and naked body. He pushed the seat back and lay there, hoping to get warm, wondering where that sound came from.

He heard a thump on the car. There was a fist banging on the side window. He shook his head and opened the door. The night air rushed in and he was awake, like escaping the ocean to breathe.

"Here," a man's voice said. "Here's your clothes."

He saw his shorts and shirt balled in the man's fist and reached for them. "Who are you?" he asked, stepping naked from the car.

Holding the clothes in the fresh night air, he felt a little new and clean, even if he couldn't stand so well. The pavement was smooth to his bare feet. He shook his head again and asked the man to turn off his car.

"Jesus, Mike," the man said, as he leaned into the car. "Are you that drunk?"

"What?" He couldn't concentrate. He was trying to balance on one leg to pull his shorts on.

"I mean are you that drunk you don't know who I am?" The man stood there, staring, as Mike fumbled with his pants and fell back onto the pavement.

"My glasses," Mike said. "I forgot them somewhere."

"Okay, alright. I'll look. You wait here."

The man closed the car door and walked to the backyard. It was Harold, their neighbour. He recognized his voice now, and frantically worked at getting dressed. He stood then, shirtless, and walked slowly and unsteadily toward the backyard.

When Harold came out he lunged at him, but he stumbled and missed. His head smashed into the edge of the gate. Harold held him and lowered him slowly to the driveway as he flailed weakly.

"Don't touch me, you goddamn . . ." he said, and passed out.

He heard voices.

"Just leave him there. He's fine."

"Look at that cut though. Jesus. We've got to take him to the hospital."

"Take you to the hospital! You need a goddamn lobotomy! I told you I'm through with him. He can take care of himself. You think that's the first time he's slept one off on the lawn?"

"Probably."

"What?"

"I live right beside you, Wendy. For years. I never saw him on— "

"Whose side are you on? I thought you—"

"What are you talking about, sides? I'm saying he's hurt and we should take him to the hospital."

"But it's out in the open now."

"He's hurt, Wendy. What has one got to do with the other?"

She was crying and he passed out again.

Someone was screaming at him. He heard her but he couldn't speak. Then she was kicking him. Her foot was in his gut and he couldn't move. He was trying to move and she kept kicking him and then she stopped. He was braced for the next blow and it never hit. There was a ringing in his head that came in waves.

He opened his eyes to see Harold carrying his wife kicking back into his house. He tried to sit up there, on the lawn, but forgot about it when he realized he was warm. There was a blanket around him and he pulled it tighter and closed his eyes again.

"Listen," a strong and quiet voice said. "You really should go. At least until tomorrow. I've never seen her so upset."

He opened his eyes and saw Harold squatting in front of him.

"I think you're way too drunk to drive, so I'll give you a ride to a hotel and then I'll take a cab home."

He couldn't believe it. Harold had always been so reasonable. He could tell anyone anything, more like an anesthesiologist than whatever he was—walking you down some small hallway to sleep.

But Mike's head was ringing and he wanted to sleep. He touched his forehead with his hand, and groaned.

"Well, you hit your head pretty good there, Mike. That's another thing. I think maybe you should go to the hospital. I think we should go there before the hotel."

"I've got to get dressed," Mike said.

"You're fine," Harold said. "Now see if you can get up."

"Wait." He threw the blanket off himself and saw that he had put his shirt on. "What are you doing here? This is still my house."

"It still is Mike, that's true. You asked me to take care of it, remember? I saw a light on and I came over and Wendy was home. It's none of my business, but I thought where's Mike? And then she heard a sound in the pool."

"No."

"Mike, I think we'd better go. Would you like a cigarette?"

Mike was sitting cross-legged now on his lawn. He took a cigarette. They sat there and smoked, facing each other.

"Sit down Harold. You make me dizzy squatting like that."

"Fair enough," Harold said, and sat cross-legged

too, though it was an effort for him. "Tomorrow is a better time."

Mike sat and shook his head. He looked at the black-green grass between them.

"What is she doing?"

"Mike, I don't know. But I think it's best if you talk about it tomorrow. I came over here and she was pretty upset finding you in the pool like that. Women—I told her when you were passed out, I said, it's his house."

"Fuck off."

"What?"

Mike glared at Harold. His head was killing him. It hurt like hell.

"I don't want you to lie to me anymore Harold. Alright?"

"I don't know what you mean."

Mike looked at his face. He looked like an elementary school principal in those big glasses, staring at Mike like he honestly was confused and hurt. His big belly stuck out from his unbuttoned shirt and his cigarette looked as small as a golf tee in his big dumb hands.

"Mike," he said, shrugging.

But Mike couldn't listen. He put his head in his hands and tried not to fall apart. His palms on his closed eyelids were cool and there was something of the sound of the ocean throughout the world right then.

"Give me another cigarette."

He took a drag of the new cigarette and realized he was crying. For once, it seemed, Harold had nothing to say. He looked at Mike like the blunt face of a cliff waiting to be climbed.

"My goddamn head hurts. My head is killing me. My wife is leaving me. My goddamn head is about to explode and my wife is leaving me and the goddamn dough-head I found her with is sitting across from me on my lawn talking to me like I'm a child. My wife is leaving me for my old goddamn lard-ass principal and my goddamn head is killing me and that principal is dead and here he is talking to me like it's a goddamn math problem I'll understand by the end of the fucking class."

Harold watched him the whole time and shook his head.

"Mike, that's not true. Not at all. As I told you, I know nothing of the trouble between you and your wife. I came over when I saw—"

Mike pulled the blanket over his head and let himself fall so he was lying on his side. He heard Harold trying to coax him to leave as he drifted off to sleep.

"The sun's coming up, Mike."

He was right. The sun, it rises every day, but Mike was never awake to see it.

"Well."

"You better go, Mike."

Mike rolled onto his side, facing Harold, and propped his head up on his arm.

"Jesus," he said. "You live right next door. I see your house right there. What are you doing here? Seriously."

Harold looked back at his house and then back at Mike and shrugged.

All the houses on the block look the same, Mike thought. The only thing different about Harold's is the little fountain in the front yard. His wife had made him build it, and the circle of rock it sat in, the summer before she had left him. It had been pathetic to watch—Harold was never any good at physical labour. It seemed like once he got working, every second movement would be to push his thick glasses back up on his sweaty nose.

Mike had to hand it to him, though; he'd done a good job.

"Harold," Mike sighed, "It's tomorrow now. I'm not going to a hotel, I'm going to sleep in my house."

He got up and walked to the front door. When he got there he turned and looked at Harold, who was crossing the lawn to his own house.

As he walked in, his wife stood glaring at him, holding an unlit cigarette in one hand and a lighter in the other.

"Don't worry," he said. "I'm going to sleep on the couch. Harold went to his house. I'm sober now. I remember everything. Leave until tomorrow, he said, over and over again. But it's already the next day. I'm too tired."

She stood exactly where she was, saying nothing.

"Harold's at his house. I don't care where you sleep. Harold's next door," he said, lying back on the couch.

Wendy lit her cigarette and stepped toward him.

"Did it ever occur to you that what he said was true? Is his story so fantastic? It could be he did come over here because I was scared—you were in the pool when you were supposed to be in Ireland."

"Didn't you hear me drive in?"

"If I heard you drive in, I wouldn't have thought it was someone else in the pool."

"I'm not stupid," he said, sitting up.

"Well, who's to say? I'm going to sleep now."

Wendy stubbed out her cigarette and was walking toward the bedroom when the doorbell rang. Mike answered it.

There was a delivery boy on the step holding some roses.

"It's six in the morning," Mike told him.

The boy looked puzzled. He checked the clipboard he was holding.

"Yes," he said, looking at his watch. "Good morning."

Mike nodded and cleared his throat.

"Well. Thank you," he said. He took the flowers and closed the door.

Wendy was standing between the kitchen and the living room. He walked over to her, watching her face. She didn't look at him. He held the flowers out to her but she shook her head.

"They're for you," he said. "Take them."

"No. I'm going to sleep," she said, but did not move.

"At least put them in some water."

"You."

"They're for you," he said, tearing the paper from around the bundle. "Six roses."

"I don't want them."

"Well, they're not for me; I'm not supposed to be here. Why six I wonder? Should I go give them to Harold?"

"Fuck you."

She looked up at him, then. What kind of way is that for her to look at me? he thought.

"Why six, I wonder?" he said again, looking dumbly at the long stems in his hand. With the paper gone they looked sharp and twisted.

"It's just a number Mike. Jesus. Why anything?"

"Well, this is how it's all happened, and here you are with roses first thing in the morning. Six. You should take them." A thorn pricked his hand and he inhaled sharply between his teeth.

"I told you. I don't want them. I'm going to sleep. You do whatever you want then go to sleep on the couch."

She turned to walk away and he screamed at her. His voice shocked them both. She turned back with a look worse than if he were dead to her.

"Fuck Wendy! They're for you!" he yelled, and threw them at her.

The flowers hit her in the face as she turned and then they fell to the floor. She stood there with her head tilted to one side. Blood trickled from a scratch on her cheek.

She looked lost, to him. She was hurt and surprised that he would hurt her. She looked like the girl he would have killed for when they were younger.

He walked into the kitchen stunned, shaking his

head and looking nowhere. He lit a cigarette from her pack on the table and sat down.

When he heard her running the water in the bathroom he imagined her washing a face full of welts. In his mind the single cut was a garish bruise, already many-coloured and full of precise incisions that would never heal. He held his head in his palms. He wanted to get up and go to her but he was too tired. Tears pooled in his hands and they tasted like sweat.

"Here," she said.

He looked up. She held a wet washcloth out to him.

"Why would I do that Wendy?"

"It's a scratch," she said, lighting a cigarette and sitting across from him.

"Not the scratch. It was the look on your face when it happened . . ."

"I'm okay," she said, looking right at him.

"Yeah, okay." He took a deep breath and tried to smile at her.

"I'm not perfect, Wendy, I'll give you that. But I never ever hurt you."

"I know."

"I wouldn't. I couldn't"

"I know Mike."

"There were times. There were times when the impulse was there, but . . . I can't forget the way you looked at me back in . . ."

"There were times for me too."

"I know. Jesus."

They watched each other across the table. It was

morning now. The sun was out. The kitchen was clean but there was a mess of roses near the door, broken and dying for water.

Mike yawned.

"Are you really leaving me?" he asked.

"I don't know," Wendy said. "But I'm tired."

"Me too, but that's no answer."

"I know."

what you need

Was it the empty room that made his voice ludicrous, or was it knowing nobody was on the other end? He hung up the phone.

Across the parking lot, thick white exhaust hung in the night air. His room faced the factory he had worked in before he left this town.

He'd been there over a year before he'd walked down the line and seen how his bit fit in. Those things were clock arms. Arms on a clock. Plastic fuckers that flipped numbers. But not here—they were shipped somewhere. The real brains put them together wherever that was. Here was just plastic and molds.

Knowing where his job fit in didn't make it better. He left anyway, afraid he would die there. Not from the plastic, not from the machines, but just from dying.

Two years ago, and now he waits in the motel, just like he and Judy agreed last week. He can't get her on the phone. Everything moves quickly. Does the boy still like the same things?

In the stack of comics at his feet the superheroes were the same as they'd ever been. The fantastic ones from his boyhood, but they cost more, and they were brighter and bigger. And there was no hero, anymore, without some kind of dark secret. You sometimes wanted one of them to be pure, still, even in this age.

He got himself a new beer. He wanted pizza but the drinking was wearing him out. A few more and he could sleep the rest of the night. He wasn't looking forward to the drive home the next day but the winter and the hangover would keep his mind off whatever wrong thing might come up.

He remembered one night long ago, when he was a child. He couldn't sleep and his father raised him to his knee where he worked at his desk.

"Your mom's not here," he said. "What's wrong?"

There was no question of safety, but the rough cheek was not his mother's. There was no question of distance, but the smell of the field was still on him, and sunlight.

He used to watch him walk up to the house as the sun set. The last thing he did every night was fill the truck to be ready for morning. Then he would come away from the long shadows of the tanks and walk with the sun behind him.

"Well, I guess that's all we'll get done today, mister," he would say as he lifted him by the arm. Then they would get into the house. He would wash in the bathroom while his father washed on the porch.

That night on his father's knee he said he didn't know if the things he saw were true. He was told they were and he believed it. He was told his mother would be home soon and she would come and tell him the same thing, if he still couldn't sleep, but he would.

Now the pressed and knotted carpet faded as he sat down on the end of the bed. The company town where he lived now didn't seem like home but neither did this.

The scale of it sometimes is what it was. You make the minute little parts. You do the tiny fucking bit. If you're lucky you're the guy at the end that ties a ribbon into a bow. But even that's not enough; what you want's the money to pay some other one to tie the bow for you but then, no, that's no good either, what you need's the money to pay to have your paying done for you.

One thing: the plastic frizzed grain of the carpet. This little room. The songs the awful, well-meaning son of a bitch just sang on TV. His warm beer. There was no fridge in the room. He thought about filling the tub with ice but, really, he'd be done soon. Warm beer is still beer.

The TV went on with its telethon. The bank of manned phones popped and clicked in the background. The man with the mic went on too.

It was the kind of thing that always got him going. Where did it end? Where does it end? Can you make a difference sending in your twenty for this little disease? Can you really make some poor fucker better? Some kid or some old one? Can they get better?

Take the ones on the screen now. They're going on and he turns the TV up. The total number behind them, over the bank of phones is digital lights, like an arena scoreboard. Not like the old days. The old days they were like numbers from a clock and real people changed them as the audience cheered the new total and the local hero, the emcee, yelled that the phones keep ringing.

His grandfather died of a disease five winters ago. It was a thing he could hardly imagine. The man had never been sick but age is age.

His boy had been eight that winter and the old man had let him sit on his lap. They talked now and then. With his watery eyes, the old man heard everything. He had lost his left arm at the elbow, long ago, in a war. The boy held the stump fondly, fidgeting, as he talked. It was a thing he had done as a baby.

And then the ride home, with the boy in the back. Later he thought of things he should have said, but at the time he was afraid more of his wife in the front than of the grandfather dying, or of the boy wanting answers.

Grandpa Bert seemed tired, he would say. Finally, his wife said, he's sick. Grandpa Bert is sick. And while she explained it, everything in the car was okay. But then the boy asked about the missing arm.

He thought it was the right time, so he explained about war. But it's the kind of thing that doesn't come out right. He tried, and he tried to tell her later that he thought it was the right thing to do.

He should have known, he knows that now. It comes out wrong. And that's why Bert was ashamed of the arm. He was afraid of how it looked. He was embarrassed. He tried to explain it once, but the gist of it, the playing dead amid the sounds and the smells of the massacre, the walking later, the trying to get help, the swinging a dead arm as you walked, the ugliness of your own body . . . "I can't word it," he had said.

And now the phone doesn't ring and the telethon

goes on. He knows he left the number and this is the hotel and he'd like to go down to the desk and say does this phone work, can you just try my room?

In the morning the exhaust in the parking lot is still there. He's in the building but sure he's breathing it in. He's listening to his ex-wife on the phone.

She says it's a mistake and sorry and did he have to leave right then. Come and have breakfast with us.

With the packing and the new information, he doesn't feel hungover. He can't decide on the comics. The TV is still on in the corner and he can't remember if the light flashing on the phone when he woke up was a message or was it the ringing?

When he gets there the boy says he's getting picked up for a basketball tournament. He's grown, for sure, and his face is awkward and changing.

"It's this that makes it worthwhile," he says, hugging the boy.

"What?" the boy asks, removing himself and bending to tie his shoe.

"Seeing you, I mean."

"Makes what worthwhile?"

"Nothing," he says, embarrassed. "I don't like my job is all."

He feels himself blush and looks at Judy and then again at the boy. She smiles a small one that doesn't make him feel stronger. He laughs and shows all his teeth to the boy.

"Ah, it's not bad. Nobody likes their job."

A car honks outside and the boy grabs his gym bag and opens the door. Brittle air wheels into the house.

"All my friends' parents have good jobs," the boy says, turning in the doorway. "Bye."

"Okay I'll call you next week," he says and turns to Judy.

"I've still got breakfast," she says. "Come and eat."

He can't answer a simple question about breakfast and he wants to get home even if that's not right either. He fishes out the comics and tells her he doesn't know if Andy still likes comics but here they are and does he?

He doesn't let go when she tries to take them, then they both let go and the comics fall to the floor.

"I should have just given them to him, even if he doesn't read them it's the thought that counts," he says, looking down.

"He'll read them, John," she says, putting her arms around him.

He thinks of all the things he thought last night. He doesn't hate her right now but he wonders is he just being taken in or is she sorry and was it all a mistake? But gas isn't cheap and he's starting to feel queasy and his car's still running and he's got a long trip.

Their faces are both red and wet and he thanks her but he doesn't know what for. His plastic footsteps in the hard snow are too loud. She says call us to say you got home safe and when he turns, at the car, she's back in the house.

we can't go on like this

The prophet came to my door this morning and told me everything was off. His hands were tied. Besides, he wanted to go somewhere warm. He looked disappointed.

I invited him in and told him what did he expect, it's a different world these days.

I've been over and over it in my mind, Pete, he said. I know everything about it. What you're saying is true.

He was depressed. I could see that. His skin was just a little paler than usual. His heart must be a little slow.

My wife, Linda, was surprised to see him. She came downstairs with a book in her hand, thinking. She seemed a bit unsure when she saw him. She was polite, but wanted to hear what he had to say. The prophet just sat looking at the space on the floor between his feet.

I told her the whole thing was off. Nothing will be done. I told her he wanted to move somewhere warm.

She was relieved, let me tell you. I could see it in her face. She was always afraid. She just didn't like the prophet's visits. It almost killed her to decide what to wear.

I had taken him aside one day and asked him not to announce his visits. I said we can't go on like this. I said we have to go to work, see friends, wash the car, and so on. I said we can just assume something will happen in the future, but we don't want it marked on the calendar.

It was a little different after that, but not much better. Linda and I, maybe we knew the patterns by then, without the appointments, without the schedule. It's one of the things that made you believe in something—this world is organic and impossible. A flat tire when you have time to change it and the nuts come off easily and your hands don't get dirty, that means nothing. But sometimes you're on your way somewhere, sometimes it takes forever and you may get sunstroke on certain days and if it's a court date that's worse.

So we knew anyway, before he would visit, but we appreciated the gesture. We felt like our business meant something.

Overall we couldn't complain. So we felt for him.

I knew what it was. It was the troublemakers. They'd come into town three months ago, sure of themselves on TV, but paler and shy in person, when you saw them in the street or buying food at the supermarket.

You might expect them to run and hug you, the way they talked on TV. You might expect them to hand out money. You might expect them to zap things with their fingers.

But the prophet didn't talk about that. He was good, to be honest. He didn't blame anyone.

Slick is what the TV guys were. Slick is what Linda called them. They're too slick, she would say, and, of course, I would agree. Fear, and all that. I was afraid, of course, but mostly it was true. They were too polished and it was easy to agree with Linda most of the time.

But they didn't have what the prophet had. It was all glass and trinkets; it was all chrome and heat.

The day we met him, we held the door for him on the way to the bank machine. We were feeling old and tired; Linda had been up most of the night—the worst night since the surgery. I had not slept well either.

The lineup was confusing. The buttons were a bit odd. I forgot my PIN number and Linda punched one in but we both knew it was wrong. The screen dissolved and reformed a number of times and I had a hard time reading it, with the sun beating in through the glazed glass, with Linda worrying we were too slow with the lineup behind us and I pushed the buttons from memory and took my card back.

The machine beeped its reminder beeps then spit from the cash slot a newborn baby, sticky and screaming. I barely held on. My reflexes are not what they used to be.

Linda pushed by me and yanked out the transaction record.

"What happened?" I asked, waiting for her to open the door. I was embarrassed, to be honest. Linda's too old to be a mother. I'll be about ninety when the kid graduates but Jesus I should be more on top of things. I was neglecting my duties. My instinct had deserted me.

Linda was caught up in the bank slip. She stood looking at it, leaving me staring at the door. I held the baby with both arms, afraid I would drop it. The prophet opened it for me and smiled. I didn't know anything about him, then, but I was struck by his graciousness.

Others in the lineup looked at me in judgment; clearly we were too old, they thought, to start on the children. They were right. The things they were thinking I was thinking too. But the prophet opened the door and with the other hand deftly snipped the baby's cord with tiny scissors that must have been palmed in his fat hand.

His beatific smile seemed to slow time. Slipping the scissors into his breast pocket he tied the cord as quickly and easily as a clown tying balloon animals.

"No," Linda said, looking at the piece of paper in her hand one more time before stuffing it into her purse. "We have to talk to them. This isn't right."

"Nonsense," the prophet said, towelling the red baby off with a soft white towel. "What a beautiful boy."

I went through a period of helplessness and confusion after the baby. I was mystified, and the prophet made a lot of sense.

Sitting at our kitchen table, he knew what to do.

"Have you gone insane?" I asked Linda. She was checking the mailbox every five minutes, waiting for the bank statement.

The prophet just shook his head and looked at the baby in his arms. I couldn't tell who he pitied: me, Linda, or the baby.

"She needs your support right now, Pete," he said, and, of course, I knew he was right.

I told him the baby stunk, what are we to do with the baby?

Pulling wet-naps and a pamper out of his pocket, he laid the baby on the table and changed it, saying first things first, the boy needs a name.

Linda was looking at him then. She'd left the front door open and glanced periodically through the screen door, still waiting for the mailman. I stood up and she was startled. I said take it easy, to make it into a joke, and smiled at her. Her face was blank and she leaned in under my arm.

"The mail's already come today," I said into her ear. "It's not coming again till tomorrow. You know that, Linda. Let's take it easy."

"Jesus, Pete," she whispered. "How can I take it easy?"

She meant the prophet, I think, more than the baby. She blamed one for the other. We looked down at the little red boy. His hands were in fists and his eyebrows moved up and down as he concentrated hard on sleeping. His lips puckered. They were the same red as the rest of his body and they sucked at each other. We were taken in, I have to admit. We were, neither of us, big fans of babies, big fans of children in general, but this one had something on us.

The prophet walked to the door and handed us the baby before he left. A lot of kids are named after dead relatives, he said.

"Linda's father was called Thomas," I said. "He died when she was seven."

"Precisely," he said, taking a comb from his pocket and running it through his hair. The slight breeze undid his work before it was done.

Linda was looking calmer. She was glad to have him out of the house, on the stoop. Thomas, Tom, Tommy. Tommy, I said, and she smiled. He'll be called Tommy.

"Perfect," the prophet said and walked to the street.

"Tommy's a good name," Linda said.

Linda got back to normal after a while. It took some time. The introductions were easy. Tommy was a big hit. People never asked where he came from. Of course, they assumed. Linda's mother was thrilled. She spent a whole week with us. At the end of it, okay, she was a stereotype and really we all were. Linda with the cooing and the anticipation of Tommy's life of good work, me with the NHL dreams, the grandmother half in tears over the future, half in tears over her long-gone husband, Linda's father, also Tommy.

The bank statement said nothing. We had money. I still went to work though I was nearing retirement. For all her waiting and all her annoyance, when it finally came in the mail, Linda read it quickly and seemed to be satisfied. It said nothing.

"I think I'll push back my retirement," I said.

The prophet nodded. You're reassessing, he said. That makes sense. I've seen it before.

The troublemakers moved into town when Tommy was eighteen and about to go to war. A lot of young men from our town signed up. Tommy would have too, but they stopped him. He became a conscientious objector.

There is no draft, we reasoned. There is no need to make such a grand gesture. We looked to the prophet for help. He had come in the morning and was getting himself a glass of water at the sink.

The prophet was no help. Tommy just smiled.

"Tomorrow morning I'll move to the house out of town," Tommy said. "They have fine facilities and I'll learn there."

I saw two little pink pills in the prophet's right hand. He swallowed them, drank the water, and leaned against the cupboard, breathing in with his eyes closed. Linda and I watched him, ready. We knew he was up to something.

"Let's see what they've got there Tommy," he said, opening his eyes. Tommy brought him the pamphlets, the forms, whatever they were. He stood with his back to the counter, he leaned back and tried to get the papers into the light from the kitchen window.

Tommy was happy, I could see that. Linda was waiting. She wanted to be happy too. She wanted Tommy to work at the factory with me, or get a job with the city maintaining the parks, or stay on one last summer on his lonely wooden tower, working as a lifeguard at the lake.

The prophet frowned at the pages. He squinted, pressed his glasses back up on his nose and held the paper right in front of his eyes.

Tommy was still smiling. He took the prophet's glasses and replaced them with thinner, lighter ones. The old guy looked sharp. He said thank you. Tommy put the old glasses in his pocket, for the underprivileged, we knew, downtown.

"This all makes good sense," he said, finally, smiling first at Tommy and then at Linda and me. Looking back at Linda, he said they seemed like a good outfit.

She shook her head and was about to get hysterical. She told the prophet he could get out of the house. I agreed, given the possible consequences and wanting the privacy of our kitchen to talk it all over.

"I'll go," he said. "I just think maybe we've misjudged them. What if we just need to look deeper?"

"They're all flash!" Linda said, screaming. "They're buzzwords with oiled hair—"

"He'll be your son," the prophet said. I could see what he was getting at and as the prophet walked down our walk and to the bus stop across the street I told Tommy to please try and understand his mother. He said I understand you both and he put his arms around her while she sobbed.

We're ninety years old, I told her yesterday, and before she could remind me she was only eighty-seven I gave her a kiss and let her in on my news. I'm quitting, I said.

She told me I should have quit years ago.

I know, I know, I said. But it hasn't been that bad.

But it was one more thing she held against the prophet. All his talk about the Bible—it makes no mention of retirement, he said. If you're doing your job, if it's your job, it is also a form of worship. Work is holy, and so on.

It's a cabinet factory, she said.

That's when he ignored her. You are a fine example,

he said to me. You are quick and sharp for your age. You build things with a smile on your face. Sometimes work is the work, the idea is the thing.

And so she shook her head and left the room. She was only civil to him after that.

This morning, we were both a bit relieved. I was tired. My hands were sore and I didn't want to ever hold a hammer again. Linda went to the door as we said our goodbyes and left the door open when she came back. She had a letter from Tommy and even showed the prophet.

He hugged her. He said none of us ever wanted him in that war.

But we, Linda especially, though maybe I flatter myself by saying so, held a lot against the prophet. He'd seen us at our low points. We'd said some terrible things, we'd had some terrible thoughts.

I, for one, did not want to work. I wanted to give Tommy up, right away. I don't include it in the story these days. These days it seems far away. But you work all your life looking for the day you can rest and, to be honest, I thought I had earned it. I didn't want the extra expense.

That time at the table I asked Linda right off. I asked her did she want to give the baby up, did she want to get in the car right now and if it took leaving him on a stoop somewhere then that's what we would do. Downtown there must be an agency.

"You can't do that," the prophet said. "You couldn't live with yourselves."

"What God are you from again?" I asked him. We had already done the introductions. I was making a point. He had already explained his secular stance, his freelance position. I wanted him to think. I wanted him to explain it again because there were holes in his story.

"Don't get snippy," Linda said. "He's from the bank. He's trying to help."

He was not from the bank, but that's where we met him. It was a confusing time. Banks employ a different sort of prophet, I explained to her. This one claimed to see a different kind of future. He made it his business to be personal and I didn't believe it. She was on his side because he knew what to do. She liked the neatly tied cord and the clean red baby relaxing in the prophet's arms.

The man kissed the baby boy on the head.

"This is a big decision," he said. "That's all I'm saying."

"We don't know who he is," I said to Linda. "This is not right."

The prophet wanted to stand. I put my hand on his shoulder and held him in his seat. I told him I was talking to my wife.

I just summarize now. I don't go much into the details. Linda wanted to know the exact figures. She waited to hear from the bank.

"We can't take the chance," she said. "If the government comes after us, we need the baby. We shouldn't give it away. Just in case."

She got worked up. The prophet told her it was ours.

"Just in case," she repeated to him. I was near tears. I was exasperated, but she made a good point.

We got on with it. We made the best. Tommy turned out pretty good.

The day the prophet said the whole thing was off, he was going away, I loved the whole world. I told that to Linda that night, and she said I'm too vague. She said don't be ridiculous.

"Get back in the house, old man," she said. "You'll have a heart attack from all this shovelling."

I was resting my arms on the shovel when Linda came back from her walk. She had red cheeks and her nose was running a little. The snow on the edge of the road was blue in the lights from the windows. It was crisp out. Believe me, the neighbourhood was quiet.

in awful repair

We hadn't been up this late for ages. It was the jet lag; we were confused. I enjoyed the look of the sky, and the textures of blue and black that made up the trees, the grass, and the road.

We had just come from a couple of weeks in Kyoto, where our daughter was. Mary kept retelling stories about our granddaughters, Megan and Madison. The way they had taught her to use chopsticks, for instance, and the things they had said as their small hands manipulated the foreign utensils without thought. I had been there too, but I liked to hear Mary talk. We were both amazed at their natural knowledge of a world so strange to us.

Years ago, she said, rolling down the window, I could not have imagined going to Japan.

I opened my window too. The night air was cool and I slowed down a bit to make the drive last.

Back then, I said, I never thought this road would be paved.

I think it's just rained, she said.

We could both smell it and breathed fully.

John, she said, back then you would have fought it. You fought everything that brought the city out here.

Well, I lost every fight, but I guess it's not so bad.

It's still the country.

We both put our windows up at the same time. One of us pressed the button to lock all the doors.

I pulled over and shut the car off. Ran out of gas, I said, holding my palms up and shrugging. Even the first time I had done that, years ago, when we were in my cousin's borrowed pickup, it had been a joke, a thing Mary's mother had cautioned her about secretly in the kitchen while I waited on the porch. She told me as soon as we were out the driveway, and we ran out of gas a lot that night.

Now she chuckled and moved to kiss me but the seatbelt stopped her. I watched her fumble with it. With all the car lights out and no one else on the road, her bones were thin and delicate, elegant, with skin as young as the night. When we finally worked our way to each other's lips, her eyes were closed. As we leaned into each other after that slow kiss, I opened my mouth on her neck, then we held each other tightly. It was to rest, after fumbling with the straps, with the console, with our cramped bodies, but it was also for my heart to slow down, for me to manage the sudden hunger I felt.

I haven't felt this way for ages, I whispered. Let's get home.

There is so much moon, she said. John, drive with the lights out?

And I did, slowly, with Mary and I silent the rest of the way, taking in whatever we could imagine the world to be beyond the road and the trees.

After we got off the paved road, we came to our lane in a couple of minutes. The driveway was a long and raised path that curved for half of a mile to our home hidden in the trees. There were lights in the lane. It took us a minute to see they were not right. It was the mood we were in, it was the nice drive from the airport. But two cars were upside down, smashed. I stopped the car by the overturned cars and turned the ignition off.

Mary said get out and look and we both did. It was natural but my heart was getting loud. The speakers in one of the cars mimicked it roughly. Things were smashed.

I'm too old for heroics, I said to Mary and she said nonsense. She held herself up against the closest car and reached her right hand out to try to stop the rear wheel spinning, as if it was an upended tricycle.

That's when she fell and her arm was snapped. I felt awful. It was the car; the rear wheels kept turning, the engine was on, the car was in gear. I knew all those things in the long moment she reached her arm out. We both felt young, being up so late, kissing in the car. But I was too slow to call out to her and her hand spun with the tire, she fell slowly into the wreck, then bounced off it. As she fell, her arm was pulled smoothly into the wheel well, then ejected—a sinister, broken shape awkward as a child's punctuation.

She lay there crying and confused in the wet grass and I went to her too fast. I fell on my knees and we all heard the bones break.

I lay down beside her. What a sight.

What a way to go. She screamed, then breathed hard to catch her breath.

She was grinding her teeth, trying not to say more. I couldn't think too well because my legs felt like they'd popped through the skin at the knees. Our faces were about a foot from each other. We just stared and tried not to blame each other, I think.

My arm's broken, she said. I just want to rest here. I could barely hear her and she flailed a bit with her good arm, then screamed at me again. It was the circumstances, I know, but it was still getting to me. Take my hearing aid out, she yelled.

I'm not the one who has trouble hearing, but she yelled it again. It's not my ears, I said, it's my arms and legs. I'm slow.

I hate that music, she yelled. Please take it out. Her good arm was pinned under her as she lay on her side; trying to move hurt her bad arm.

By then I had shoved myself up on one elbow. But that was hard. That took time and no matter how I moved it was like grinding my knees into the ground. I reached over the best I could.

Like trying to pick a dime up on a marble floor, it was, with no fingernails. You never think of it but Jesus my fingertips could not fit close to the holes of her ears. I've got thick fingers. I jammed the one pinky in there and tried my best to dig. It took all I had to try.

Mary's face crinkled up and I knew it wasn't right so I just leaned forward to rest. My forehead was wet with sweat and I was close to Mary. I wanted to lay down and hold her.

Just wait there, Mary, I said. I can't do it. I'll try again.

Just then, a young man so pale he looked bright against the dark night stumbled up.

Hey, I don't know you, he said, and sat down on the edge of the road, facing us.

Listen, son, I said. Go get help. There's been an accident.

He told us he knew that, and looked at us puzzled. You're arm is badly broken, he told Mary.

The whole time he sat there he didn't blink. He told us he was tired. He said there'd been a party, he'd loved a girl called Karla, he didn't know what to do about the cars, or any of the rest of it. They had all gotten carried away. They had gone too far. Everything was over.

Everything will be fine, Mary yelled at him. Go take our car and go up to our house—

Nothing is fine. She's dead. I checked. I tried to save her and I got her blood in my mouth. He held his head in his hands. He went on, loudly. This is Karla, he said. I love her and she's dead. Tonight, I think she liked me. She was sitting right beside me, even when there was room to move away. She was amazing in the dash-lights.

He was in shock. He didn't hear us and sunlight was starting to creep into the sky. The engine of the one car kept running. The music kept throbbing and Mary cried behind me quietly, as I alternately tried to rise, and listened to that boy.

The sun coming up reminded me of an old movie. In it, some culprits hid in a ditch. It had only been a movie, but still, I remembered it with the smell, and with the feel. The grass felt like this grass—chilly and long. There was pollen in the air, somewhere.

One thing was different though. In the movie there was the smell of smoke. It was the way they cut now and then to various scenes—flashbacks to the two villains lighting the fire; shots of the horse's wild eyes and flaring nostrils, their manes moving in the wind and in their anxiousness, as smoke would, if it were visible; and the delicate woman inside the coach waking and becoming alarmed.

The man riding shotgun must have been drunk not to notice. Drunk, or in on it.

The pale boy had a dark smear on the right side of his face. He reached first into one car, then into the other. The music was stopped and the wheels stopped turning. An engine coughed and was silent.

The silence was confusing. I had to get my bearings. Mary always said my memory was going. I changed the subject but I knew she was right and it scared me. I can remember the names of the grandchildren, Megan and Madison, but I can't remember their faces or their voices. I have no control. I remember scenes, from lives or from movies. I find myself forgetting I am old. In the darkness I believed Mary and I were young again. I have to grasp onto details, like electric locks, electric windows, new pavement that has been there for twenty years.

What a relief, Mary said. She put her head back on the ground. I hadn't realized how hard she'd been straining.

The boy wandered slowly, away from our house. With the sunrise, you couldn't see the yard light anymore.

I started to call to him, but my throat needed clearing.

What is it? Mary asked.

I watched the boy sink to his knees. It was nothing like movies; he carefully laid himself down there on the gravel road and drew his knees up close to his chest.

I watched him fumble around with his eyes closed, trying to find a blanket he imagined, his slackening body settling onto the hard surface of the road.

Well, Mary, I said.

What?

I think it's up to us.

What? She still didn't open her eyes.

The boy's almost dead, I said. He can't get help.

Oh, she said, opening her eyes and trying to smile. Well, it's only my arm.

And the general pain.

And the general pain, she agreed, and almost laughed.

For me, I said, I think something's wrong with my legs.

Black humour, it's called. I've seen it also in movies. The hero wrestles with a dilemma and then tosses some joke off after saving the woman. It tells them both they haven't lost their humanity, which, given some of the obstacles, and some of the evil, is all the triumph they can hope for.

In the western I had been reminded of, all sorts of jokes were made as they went along. When the culprits were found out, it was only by our woman in the coach, with her heightened sensibilities. She asked the driver to stop, and he did. Beside him the guard dozed with the shotgun. Or did he? In the darkness, and light of the movie lanterns, you could almost, for one second, see his eyes open slightly, and a small smile on his face.

You never know who's in on it.

In another western, the story begins with an undertaker riding with his cart down the main street. The road is in awful repair. He hits a bump. He's going quite slowly, but this is 1890 and it's just a nailed-together cart, so the coffin clatters onto the ground.

This is a sequel to the one I remembered earlier. This one was made decades later. In it, one of the original culprits has been killed. The other has disappeared. He might be dead, or he might be terrorizing some other small town. They have lasted a long time. It was surely the point where age may have gotten them too.

When the coffin falls to the ground, there is apprehension all around. Will the coffin open? Two characters we will know later watch it fearfully. It stays shut, thankfully.

I say thankfully because everyone knows who is in there and they aren't sure he is dead. They had seen the gunfighter killed, most of them, but still. You wonder. You can't help it.

Nobody would help the undertaker lift the coffin. It stayed in the street for most of the movie.

I had to drag myself to the car. Ten years earlier I'd had surgeries on my knees. I knew that work had been undone. Mary did her best to help me, opening the car door with her good arm. I couldn't look at the wrecked one. If it hurt me to see it I knew the pain was almost unbearable, with it hanging there, with the blood flowing down to it.

When I was in the car I put it in drive and we rolled slowly to our house. Mary was in the back. I couldn't press the pedals. We came up slowly to an awful scene. I put the car in neutral, and then into park.

Our yard was a mess. The lawn was welted with tire tracks—muddy dark ruts intersecting and curling in circles and sharply ended lines. As the sun came up the scene verged on beautiful; the short, manicured lawn was lopsided but motionless, and its green looked impossible against the black earth turned up inside it.

What's happened? we both asked together.

The front windows were smashed. The bedroom TV sat alone beside the cracked birdbath, its cord beside it in the cursive loop of a cat's tail, lazy and still, but suggesting motion.

The whole scene was peaceful. The front door was wide open, and the piano had one leg out the door.

I thought Mary might faint. She heaved herself out of the car and said she'd go in and phone. I collapsed on the front seat. I said Mary, I'm sorry, I can't move, but she was already gone and I closed my eyes.

What have I done? I thought to myself. What have I let Mary in for? Whoever had done this could still be in there. There is no way to tell. Lying on the front seat staring at the roof of the car, I couldn't move. The silence stretched time, and my poor legs hurt with each beat of my heart. It was time ticking off in my body, reminding me that Mary was gone into our wrecked house and I had sent her there, crawling under the piano, doing her best to hold one poor arm. She had gone in and she would be gone for a long time.

Birds chirped this morning. I pictured them puzzled on their dewy branches and closed my eyes. The sound they made was like the signal to cross the street in the foreign city we'd just left. I wanted to hurry but I could not move.

taxi

The taxi was like any other on the slushy roads; dirty on the outside, clean but old on the inside. The back seat was cramped. He sat in the middle. On his left was a crate with her dog in it. She sat on his right.

He got out of the taxi and she told the driver keep driving.

Getting out was hard because he was in the middle and it was either over her or the dog in the crate and she was not cooperating.

She told the driver keep driving and she pulled the dog crate toward her. Tears began in her eyes. You must see the stupidest things in cabs, she said. The taxi driver nodded politely.

He left the taxi and looked around smiling. When he'd met her, she'd mistaken his smile for confidence. Lately she'd seen him smile too often and realized it was out of fear. He smiled when there was nothing else to do.

She made the driver circle the block and saw him again by the newspaper box where he'd been dropped.

He looked at the taxi and watched it move on. He wasn't smiling anymore. It was his one expression and now he was expressionless as he looked down at his feet.

When he got out of the taxi and she told the driver

keep driving, his right foot was wet where he'd stepped in a puddle. It was spring, but it was still cold.

He looked at the newspaper in the box and took it all in. Someone was suing somebody somewhere. Well, right here in this city where she had moved them. He lived here but he still didn't know the people in the paper.

She drove back around and asked the taxi to stop.

His back was to her and he read the headlines without understanding. His head was clouded. His briefcase had enough in it, he ought to know where to go, but he didn't.

You see this all the time, don't you? she said to the driver. He smiled politely and tapped the meter. Her makeup was running and when she saw herself in the mirror, she felt her nails were as long as knives as she pulled hair from her face. This is not about money, she wanted to scream.

It hadn't been easy to get out of the taxi and he stood and wondered where to go next. His feet ached from the cold. It was arthritis. The doctors told him the cold wouldn't matter. But it did.

She had felt so strong in the morning, watching him smile in his sleep. She woke him up and they embraced. With everything settled, she took a deep breath, then they marched right out and hailed a cab.

He stared at the headlines and lit a cigarette. She looked at his back.

The driver said what are you going to do? and the dog barked and he turned around and saw her and she said keep driving.

prayer

"Can't read it anymore," he said, holding the paper up to the sky, even though it was night.

Jenny squinted at the loose-leaf James held with both hands. With her hands on his shoulders, she turned him to face the light from the door. It made the blurred ink even harder to read; now they saw blue smudges on both sides at once.

"Jesus," she said. "What did you do to it? Is that sweat?"

"It was in my sock. You know what it's like in there. I sweat like a pig all night."

"But why was it in your sock?"

"You gonna give me a smoke or what?" he asked as he turned to face her. "I'm not standing out here for your fucking company."

They shivered. Jenny handed him a cigarette and took one for herself.

"Bring your own sometime."

"Fuck you. You bum from me all the time."

The night was black and clear around them. They stood in a patch of light that came from the open kitchen door of the restaurant where James worked. For the past two nights Jenny had been coming over to the restaurant during her break. She hadn't been able to keep a job for a long time. Then she had gotten this position at the inventory company. Her first job with the new company turned out to be at the mall where the restaurant was. Things were going well for her. For them.

They huddled together to light the cigarettes, but the wind in the alley blew each match out. He looked at her cold red face and loved her.

He shoved her inside and closed the door behind them. "I'm smoking in here tonight," he said, stamping the snow from his shoes.

He grabbed two empty milk crates and walked toward the bags of flour and sugar stacked in the back of the kitchen. She followed him and sat on the first crate. He turned to go get them coffee.

"Wait. Let me see the paper," she said.

He threw it to her and went.

She lit the cigarette and looked at the paper. She could make some of the words out, but not many.

James handed her a coffee, sat down, and lit his cigarette.

"Well, what do you think of that?" he asked. "It's a prayer, I think. Some sort of good-luck, rabbit's-foot prayer."

"If it's a good-luck kind of thing, maybe it's a mantra or something. I don't think those are two pages long."

"I know. It's a prayer though."

"Anyway, I can't tell. It's too smudged."

"Yeah but here's what it was like," He took a drag

from his cigarette. He followed along, pointing to the words on the page as if he could still read them, and told her what it had said before it was unreadable.

"You are a fat tub of lard. You have no friends because you are mean and you whine. There is no one to blame but you. You stink and you will always be weak and fat. You—"

"That doesn't sound like a prayer, James."

"True, true," he said. "But it went like that for a few lines and then it would say stuff like 'I deserve everything I have. I am a good person. People love me because I am a kind, strong person.'"

He took a sip of coffee and looked at her. "Well, it was stuff *like* that, not exactly that." He shook his head and laughed. "I guess a person can feel pretty shitty sometimes, but . . . so someone wrote this down. 'I'm bad, I'm good, I'm bad, I'm good' and on and on. It's funny so I was trying to get a look at whoever—"

"Why'd you take it?" she frowned.

"There was this woman," James said. He was still laughing. "I think it was her because, I don't know, she wasn't fat or anything but it seemed like her eyes were too open all the time, like she's just been slapped and, you know, her hair was dyed but it—"

"Fuck James! Why'd you take it?"

He looked at her, puzzled, and stopped laughing. She was staring at him, not with anger, but like he was some type of insect or machine that defied the physical laws she knew.

"What? I didn't mean to. I thought it was money."

They had talked about that before. The customers' coats were hung right inside the door of the restaurant. James walked by them when he came to work and sometimes he would stick his hand in a pocket and take what loose money was there.

"Why'd you think it was money?" She grabbed the paper from him. "It's bigger than money. It doesn't *feel* like money. Why the hell ya gotta take money anyway?"

"You always tell me what to do. Do I tell you what to do?"

Jenny lit another cigarette.

He went on: "Look. If they've got money in their coat pocket and they leave it—"

"Yeah yeah. I know. It's like money in the couch. They already forgot they have it. Whatever. But why'd you think it was money?"

"You know what? You're making me nervous." He shrugged. "I'm nervous."

"You're nervous taking the money."

"I'm not nervous taking the money—I'm nervous *when* I'm taking the money."

"Because it's stupid," Jenny said.

"It's stupid to be nervous."

"It's stupid to steal the money."

"See—that's how you make me nervous. Nobody ever noticed any money missing. It's just luck anyhow; there usually isn't any money in the pockets I check. I probably took fifty bucks over the last two years. Who misses it? But now—"

"Now you're nervous," she said.

"Yeah. Now I'm kinda fumbly. So I couldn't tell, so I took this fucking thing." He grabbed the paper from her. "I thought you might get a kick out of it. Sorry."

"I better go," Jenny said.

They stood and walked to the door. She had her back to him as she did up her coat.

"Are you guys done in this mall, or will you still be here tomorrow night?" James asked.

She turned toward him and looked in his eyes and then to the floor.

"There's still some work here, I guess." She said it so quietly he moved closer.

"Alright. I'll see if I can steal you a sandwich or something tomorrow."

"But I don't think I'll be here." She bit her lip.

He reached out to her and pulled her head to his shoulder. She squeezed him, and let out a sob. He felt the words in her breath on his neck, more than heard them. "They say I can't do it James they say it's wrong and I was trying and they say it's not good and I try and—I know, I can see how it works and I try and it's simple. If I can't do this simple job . . ."

He pulled her head up and kissed her wet face.

"Okay," he said. "It's good. You can get a daytime job. It's good. Night work fucks people up."

She wiped her nose with her mitt.

"I better go," she said, and turned back to the door. "Wait."

"It's okay," she said. She looked over her shoulder and gave a small smile as she pushed on the door. "Can we talk at home?"

He nodded and she turned and pushed again at the door, this time with both hands. It was too heavy. He stepped around her and threw all his weight into it. It opened and she walked out dressed for winter.

James closed the door and turned back to the kitchen. It was work just to remember all he had to do before morning.

the way it happened always

Abraham made Isaac carry the wood for the sacrifice. He himself carried Isaac, who was just a boy, in the beginning.

But the boy grew and the man became tired.

Why aren't you eating? the boy asked.

I am, the man said. Look.

He put food in his mouth and chewed. It was tough to take though. His mind was elsewhere.

I'll tell you why, the boy said.

The man shook his head. He was old, but old is relative.

You don't know, he said. What do you know? You're young. Sometimes a man has things to do he can't possibly do. Sometimes a man speaks to his son without a thing to say, because that's the way—a man speaks and a son listens.

The son watched his father. You're too hard on yourself,

he said in his deepening voice.

The old man bit off some bread and stared at the one talking to him.

It's tough, he said. I'm getting older. I remember when God speaking was the way it happened always. Do you think I don't know it's not done anymore?

He stretched out and lay on his back, looking to the sky.

You're too hard on yourself, the young man said again. It's just a story, he said, holding a glass of water to his father's lips.

The old man reached up and felt the other's face. Isaac? he whispered.

The young man ignored his name.

Come on, he said, we still have miles to go.

But the old man was deaf. There was no way for the young man to explain, so he ignored the questions and led his ancient father home.

we'll keep an eye out

Joey and Adam watched the old man, who sat in his living room.

"What's he doing?" Joey asked.

"Can't tell," Adam said.

"Look how slow he moves."

"My mom said he never washes his clothes. She had to go talk to him once and she couldn't breathe, she said."

The old man raised himself in stages from the couch, then slowly moved toward another room. At the edge of where they could see him, he bent down and picked something up. They couldn't tell what.

Joey took a spoon from his pocket and hit Adam on the head. Adam yelped and pushed Joey over. They were roughly the same size but Joey was meaner. He probably brought the spoon just to hit Adam. Just as Adam pulled it from Joey's hand, the door to the old man's house opened, and they were silent, except for the scurrying to get back out of sight.

The old man held a small wooden stake with a cardboard sign on it. They couldn't see what it said and he dropped it face down on the lawn by the step. He walked down the sidewalk toward the garage.

The street's pavement was smooth and soft in the summer's heat.

Adam watched him move with one eye. He held the cup of the spoon over his other eye. Joey watched the old man for a moment too, then tried to smash the spoon-covered eye with his little fist. Adam was too quick. He pulled the spoon away and held it up to the sun with a flourish.

"Ta da!"

"Give it to me."

"It's mine now."

"Adam you don't understand. I'm in deep shit if I don't take it back."

"Shhhh!" The man was coming back out. "You should've thought of that," Adam added quietly.

The man held a long-handled sledgehammer in his hand and walked a bit more quickly than usual. He used the hammer as a cane sometimes. He wore a greying under-shirt and banged the sign into his lawn very quickly for such a slight man, and surely. It said only "For Sale." What made Adam and Joey imagine the sign would have a message?

His pants were too large. He smiled when he squint-ed in the sunlight. He might have winked at one of them.

"Mr. Kashul's selling his house," Adam's mother said at supper that night.

"Why's that, I wonder," Adam's father had said.

His mother had gestured to the right with her fork, making small circles, then pointed to her filled cheeks. She continued to chew and by the time she was done they had forgotten the topic. They both looked to the side and down. His father's gaze in this way fell on Adam.

He smiled and asked how his day had been. Adam said fine and took a drink of milk.

"What did you do?" his father asked.

"Just hung around with Joey," Adam said.

"You must have had a hard day," his mother said to his father.

"What did you and Joey do?" his father asked, ignoring his mother.

"Nothing, really," Adam said.

"Listen to this," his father said to his mother. "His day was fine. He did nothing all day with Joey."

"We made up a game with this spoon," Adam said. Looking at his mother he added "We found a spoon out in the gutter."

"This meat is pretty tough," his mother said. "I planned supper for a bit earlier."

"It's fine," his father said, waving his knife, dismissive. He took a drink from his glass, burped loudly and smiled over at Adam. "It's great."

The next morning Adam hid the spoon in his sock when he dressed. The more secrets the better. He left the house and was going to walk over to Joey's, but Joey was standing in front of Kashul's house, not even trying to hide.

"The sign's gone," he said to Adam.

He was right. They could see the small brown lesion on the lawn where the sign had been pounded through and then pulled up sometime, violently.

"Where's Kashul?" Adam asked.

Joey looked at him and shrugged. "What?"

"The old man's name is Kashul."

"How do you know?"

"My mother told me."

"He's not on his couch yet."

They stood casually, with their hands in their pockets, like two older men waiting for a job to start.

"We could go around the back and see him," said Joey, rubbing his nose.

"Where?"

"In his backyard, I guess."

"Is he there?"

"He's in the kitchen, I bet," Joey said.

"Oh," Adam said. "Breakfast."

"Right."

"Or maybe he's dead."

"What?"

"Maybe he knew and that's why he sold the house."

"Yeah, that's right," Joey said, his eyes widening. "People can tell. I saw it in a movie."

"Right, and when my grandpa died my dad knew."

"Yeah because you and your mom went to America to see him."

"He must have known," Adam said, gripping Joey's shoulder. "He called my dad you know."

"Of course he knew. So did this old guy."

They decided to go to his backyard and try to see him. There were gardens in the backs of the houses on that side of the street, held in by retaining walls. The gardens were higher than the back windows of the houses, so the two boys crept on their stomachs through rows of peas and carrots.

As they lay in the dirt looking through low rows of green, they saw the old man in the kitchen. He was sitting at the table with a mug in front of him. He had a marker and he was concentrating on a piece of cardboard in front of him, moving his right hand slowly, writing, at times holding it steady with his left hand.

"Some kid must've taken the sign," Joey said.

"Probably a teenager," Adam said.

"What would they do with it?"

"I don't know."

They lay there and thought about that.

"This kid at school, his brother goes to Sir George Simpson," Adam told Joey. The school was notorious for many things. They heard about it all the time, from other kids, and they were secretly scared to grow older and go there.

"I know someone who goes there, too," Joey said.

"This kid's brother's bald now. They sprayed him with Neet."

"What's Neet?"

"My mom uses it. It's like spray paint but you can't see it and it takes your hair off."

"Like acid?" Joey asked.

"Exactly."

"Why?"

"There was no reason. They sprayed him all over and he didn't even know the kids."

"Were they taking drugs?"

"Probably," Adam said.

When they were crawling back out, Joey lobbed a dirt lump onto Adam. It startled him and he jumped up and ran. They both did; they knew they were too fast and would be gone long before Mr. Kashul could look up and see them.

When they were back out on the street, a few houses over, Joey held up the spoon smugly.

"I found this in your sock," he said. "Lucky for you my mom didn't notice."

"That's not all she didn't notice last night," Adam said, and started running.

Joey didn't know what it meant, but he knew it wasn't right, so he ran after him.

Every day the old man put a sign up, and every morning there was no sign. Adam and Joey had other things to do, but this problem occupied their imaginations when they weren't at the swimming pool, or shopping with their mothers or riding their bikes over the newly stripped lots on the next block.

A hole was dug and a foundation poured in the new lots. It was just after supper and they sat with their backs to the smooth concrete. They had been thinking of jumping in but didn't know how they would get back up.

"What do you think was buried here?" Adam asked.

Joey was silent.

"Indians?" Adam asked.

"Maybe."

"Tomahawks, I bet."

"Yeah. I bet that's true. Where do they go?"

"They probably go to the museum, I guess," Adam said, tying his shoe.

"There are no tomahawks there."

"Oh, but maybe now there are."

"You know what we should do?" Joey said, hitting Adam on the shoulder.

"Go to the museum?"

"What? No. We should be here next time."

Adam looked at him and finished tying his shoe. Joey was excited. Usually his ideas were for things that would happen the very next second.

"What for?"

"We watch them and we see something they don't and maybe we can just have it."

"Yeah, yeah. They use pretty big machines. Maybe they don't notice all the stuff."

They decided many things happened when they weren't around and the idea was then to be around more often. It carried over to the old man's sign. They decided to watch it all day one day, and see what happened.

Joey slept over at Adam's one night. They were going to get it right. They snuck upstairs in the dark to the empty guest room and waited. They could see the television's light in the living room, but they could barely see the sign.

"Jesus Adam, you stink," Joey said, waving his hand in front of his nose.

"I know," Adam said, laughing.

A small car drove up the street and pulled up in front of Kashul's house. They saw the face of a tired woman in the lights of the dash. The woman got out of the car in stages, angry and shaking her head.

She pulled the sign out of the lawn and walked up to the house, where she let herself in with a key. The house lit up room by room. Joey and Adam saw shadows, one moving slowly and one flapping its arms in the air.

The next day the same woman came to see Adam's mother.

"He's just making a show," Adam heard her say. She had a nervous voice, deeper than his mother's but not as smooth. She laughed a lot, quickly and briefly.

"I understand," his mother said.

"He can't do yardwork anymore. He's got to be careful and now he doesn't want to stay."

"Well, I could mow the lawn, from time to time."

"Thanks. But I suggested getting someone to do it. He won't hear of it."

"It's tough getting old," his mother said. There was silence, then she added, "My father died a couple of years ago . . ."

"He wants to sell the house and have no yard. I know he would go mad."

"In a home?"

"No. He's sure about that. Not a home. But where, then? I asked him."

Adam saw from the hallway his mother was getting uneasy. The woman stared at her with her eyes wide, trying to smile.

"Is there anything I can do?" his mother asked finally.

"Oh, sorry. Sorry. I do have a small favour. It's tiny. Probably unnecessary.

"It's fine. Ask away."

"It's just, can you keep a look out? I mean, it won't happen, but if someone comes by to look at the house."

"Of course."

"He's just so vulnerable. Anything could happen. Even if he could sell it, his prices are probably stuck in 1952. Sometimes he makes no sense."

"We'll keep an eye out," his mother said, patting the woman on the shoulder.

Adam went back to the kitchen and spooned some cereal into his mouth. What did he learn and what will he tell Joey? They already knew the old man was crazy, but what if he had a heart attack someday while they hid in the bushes? They had better watch him carefully and call 911 when it happened.

He wasn't listening and all of a sudden heard the woman's wet voice rise as she breathed hard from crying.

"Even pounding the sign in. It's *physical.* He's not supposed to do it. He *knows* that."

Adam raced out to the hallway. The shining eyes of the woman looked right at him as Adam's mother held her and patted her back.

"Who knows what could happen?" the woman said quietly and closed her eyes.

One evening, they were out by the new houses, playing x's and o's on the pavement with scraps of gyproc, when they suddenly looked up.

The old man was walking toward them on the sidewalk. He shielded his eyes with one hand before each step, then lowered the hand slightly as he moved forward, as if he needed it to balance. It seemed as if he saluted the setting sun with each step.

"That's Kashul," Joey said.

"I know. What's he doing?"

"Let's ask him."

"No!" Adam hissed. "Remember, he's crazy!"

But it was too late. Joey was walking up to the old man.

Adam stood but didn't know if he should follow. When he saw the old man keep walking while Joey talked, he decided to wait for them.

"I live next door," Joey was saying, as they walked up to Adam. "And this is Adam, he lives across the street."

Mr. Kashul stopped and held out his hand, which Adam shook silently.

"This day sure went fast," the man said, with his hands on his hips. "I've got to sit down."

Joey pulled a cinderblock from the dirt onto the sidewalk.

Mr. Kashul took a small trowel out of his back pocket and lowered himself onto the cinderblock.

"Is that a knife?" Joey asked.

"No, it's a bit like a knife."

"What is it?"

"It's a trowel." The boys watched the old man turn it in one hand, then lay the blade flat in the other hand. "It's a small one, though. I built my house with my bare hands, you know. I did everything."

"Mine was built ever since I can remember," Joey said.

Adam had pulled a spoon from his pocket and held it by the handle as he watched the old man.

"Well, you're just a boy."

"Where's your big trowel?" Joey asked.

"I don't know. This one is awful small. What would it be for?"

"Is it yours?"

"It was right by my kitchen sink but I don't know what it's for. My daughter, she moves things around and buys stuff and sells stuff . . ."

Joey said "Wow," and Adam looked at him, puzzled.

It was the old man's hand. The tip of one finger was missing.

"What happened to your finger?" Joey asked.

"Don't ask that!" Adam said, hitting Joey on the shoulder.

"That's okay," Mr. Kashul said. "It's from the old days, that's all."

The boys watched him. He rubbed one eye with his shortened finger.

"But how did it happen?" Joey asked

"I don't want to talk about that," he said. "But it works fine." He wiggled the finger's stump in Adam's face and Joey laughed.

"Well, if that happened to me," Joey said, "I could never forget what happened. Adam broke his arm last summer and I couldn't believe it. It was gross."

"I remember what happened. I just don't want to talk about it."

"That's okay, Mr. Kashul," Joey said, putting his hand on the old man's shoulder. "Some people forget things anyway but I know what it's like not to want to talk about it. Adam's grandpa died and nobody wants to talk about anything anymore. Right Adam?"

It was true. Adam had forgotten he'd told Joey about it. His parents had changed. But he looked at the old man's smile and couldn't say anything. His teeth were false. Adam wanted to ask him to do the trick his grandpa had done with his false teeth.

"He's a bit shy," Joey said, and Adam blushed.

"That's alright. We're all different. I do forget things, you know. But right now I'm just tired. I'll sit here for a bit and talk with you boys."

Joey told the man about his own grandpa, whom he knew only from stories. Mr. Kashul talked about his daughter and how she worries too much.

The ice cream truck drove up. Adam heard it approaching from a couple of blocks away, but he wasn't sure if Joey and Mr. Kashul heard. Of course it was impossible not to hear the truck's music, but they showed no sign.

As the truck slowed, though, Joey jumped up suddenly.

"I've got an idea," he said to the old man. He dusted off his pants and walked up to the window of the truck.

"Can you give this man a ride home?" he asked, pointing back with his thumb. Before the woman driving the truck could speak, Joey went on: "He's tired because he's had a long day. His name's Mr. Kashul and he lives right beside my house, which is 474."

As the boy spoke, the old man sat happily on his cinderblock. It seemed that either possible answer would be fine with him. He rubbed his cheek with the back of one hand, then started to rise.

The woman leaned out the window, looking both ways down the street.

"There are no customers," Joey said. "Mostly my friends are on holidays."

"Well," the driver said, "do you want a ride?"

The old man pulled himself up, resting his hand on Adam's shoulder to steady himself.

"Sure," he said.

He got in the truck and it pulled away, leaving the boys watching it. They forgot their chalk games on the pavement and walked toward home.

Adam told Joey he knew what happened to the finger. He knew it must have been in the war, or else maybe in construction. Maybe the old man used to be a farmer. People are always getting hurt by machines.

"He's lucky he didn't lose his whole arm," Joey said.

"Yeah. My uncle's cousin was killed by a tractor rolling over on him."

They rounded the corner and saw a woman talking

to the ice-cream lady by Kashul's house.

"That's the daughter," Adam said. "She came to my house. She's the one who said watch out for the old man."

"Not watch out, but help him, right?" Joey asked.

"Yeah."

When they got a bit closer they stopped and watched. The women finished what they were saying and the truck drove off. That's when they saw Mr. Kashul standing on the step.

"The goddamn door's locked!" he yelled.

"It was wide open when I came," his daughter said. "I had to lock it. Anyone could have walked in."

"I was only gone a minute."

"Well, you should lock it and take a key with you. It's not like it used to be—there are people all over. You've got to be careful."

"I am careful. Now open the goddamn door!"

She walked up and unlocked the door for him, then stood waiting for him to go in. He shoved her on the shoulder.

"Get in! I'm not an invalid!"

It was only a week or so later when Adam's family came home one day to find Joey waiting on their steps.

"They took Mr. Kashul away in an ambulance," he said to Adam.

"That's awful," Adam's mother said. "When?"

"Yesterday," Joey said.

Adam's father carried suitcases from the car and

tried awkwardly to get around the people on the steps before dropping the bags on the lawn and going back to the car.

"What happened?" Adam's mother said.

"It's a stroke, my dad said . . . I think."

"Is he alright?"

"I don't know."

Adam's mother looked over at Kashul's lawn and muttered something. Sometimes she prayed if her husband couldn't hear her. Sometimes she just moved her lips.

"Come on," Adam's father said, returned and loaded down again. "Move into the house."

Adam took his mother's keys and opened the door. His mother walked a couple of steps away from the house and Joey walked with her. Adam took a bag and followed his father in.

"What's got into your mother?" Adam's father asked.

"Mr. Kashul's in the hospital."

His father put his hands on his hips and looked out the screen door. "Hmm," he said. "No lights on, and no sign on the lawn, it must be true." Then he picked up his suitcase and walked to the bathroom.

"Can you bring in the rest, Adam?"

"Sure."

The next night Joey stayed over. They kept watch on the old man's house, but nothing was going on.

Some time later, the summer days already seemed shorter.

Joey and Adam had been inside their houses watching TV but met at the ice cream lady's truck. As she drove away, they noticed lights on in the Kashul house.

They ate their creamsicles in the diminishing light, sitting on the curb with their jackets on. Lights from houses revealed televisions and empty living rooms. Small conversations came from the backyards along with the sounds of ice cubes in glasses and occasional shots of hard laughter.

The garage door at Kashul's began to roll up, and pale light spread down the driveway as it opened. The old man's daughter sat on a riding mower and waited for the door to stop moving. There were dark smears under her eyes and they knew she was crying by the way her body moved in the seat.

The light strokes of its engine sounded as she started the small tractor and drove out onto the old man's lawn; it was the perfect warm drone of a new machine. She wheeled around the outside edge, circling in. They could only see the dark shape of her outside the garage's light. The mower's engine stopped, creating a new silence over the street. Now the old man's daughter leaned forward and rested her head on the steering wheel.

She stayed that way while the boys chewed the wooden sticks from their ice cream and the lights went out two doors down. They weren't startled when Adam's father came out and whispered to them to get home, though they hadn't heard his steps, and they hadn't heard the sound of a door.

something I learned from the news

I got pretty close to him. There was a lot of pushing, but it seemed polite enough; once every person had held his hand and smiled, and received his smile back, they fell away and let him pass.

I was in the crowd, and I guess I moved with them, so that it came my turn to greet him, and I did, and I smiled despite myself. He was so large and the day was damn hot, but he moved with such ease through the heat and crowd. But those eyes were freaky. I don't believe in him, but he's doing something right.

I read in the paper there were two hundred people there to see him, but it seemed like more to me. Especially on TV. The paper said some other things like he was not a faith healer and he wasn't someone who had formed a new church or a cult. But it didn't really say what he was. Actually, after reading a bit of the story I only scanned the rest to see if it would say something about his eyes. It didn't and I don't know why. I think those eyes are nuts, just like I think he is—I think he *should* run a cult. But there's something wrong with me. I am afraid of blue eyes. They seem sort of evil or something—they're from Satan somehow.

I saw a guy's eyes turn blue once. We were in this

little field. It was a barnyard, and there was a horse there. It was a crippled horse, but it could still walk. We were staking the route of a new pipeline and it went by the corral this horse was in. It wasn't really crippled—I guess it just walked funny. But when we got there, the horse was lying on the ground and its stomach was huge and heaving. There was a rope around its neck to tie it to the fence and it was choking. So John cut the rope at the horse's neck and it got up. It just shook its head a bit and ran around a little, the best it could. But John, he just stood there, leaning on the fence and staring right through the horse and he was crying.

And his eyes were blue for some reason and he wasn't looking *at* anything. They didn't stay blue, but blue eyes still bug me. And this cult guy had one blue eye. And it looked kind of to the right and a little up. And the other one, the brown one, it definitely looked straight down. Or, more down than straight.

I got home and I forgot about it. I just watched some TV and made something to eat. Actually, I did think about him when I was making the food. I tried to, I sort of put my left eye down a little and tried to move the other one away too, to try and think about how the cult guy would make macaroni. I quit when I hurt my hand in the steam of the boiling water. It burned so I forgot about the eye thing and said shit or something and went to watch TV.

There was some type of movie on but I was flipping around and then the news came on and the cult guy was on there. Well, the crowd around him was on—it was difficult to see him there.

But I saw the gun. I mean, I saw him and I saw the gun that got him, but it was all grainy.

It was home video. I remember, because there were some people with those cameras there. I remember when I left there were all these people pointing cameras away from me at, I guess, the guy with the funny eyes. I saw he was just lying there. There must have been blood.

Those cameras piss me off. There are always more people shooting than doing anything to be shot. So I left, because at my parents' house in the winter I just want to watch TV and my parents and sisters just film everything those little kids do and I am always getting in the shot. And I can't watch TV—they want me to get out of the way and then they want to watch the video they just shot.

John was with us once. The guy whose eyes turned blue, he was with us at my parents' house. He's about forty-five or so. This was only a week before that happened with his eyes. He'd never been out west before, but his wife had died recently. He never saw his son anymore and he was moving to BC to stay with his daughter. I always forget her name. Anyway, nothing good ever happens to John. He lives the best he can, but everything bad happens. His daughter was killed in a car accident and he didn't want to go to BC anymore. He stopped by our house in Asquith and the pipeline was just starting so he got a job there with me.

A guy who lost all that shouldn't smile so much, I thought. But he loved my nieces and nephews and he was always smiling. Nothing had ever really happened, I guess, to look at him. We've still got all those tapes.

I guess there must be hundreds of people with tapes of the cult guy getting shot. I've got one with stories from a bunch of different newscasts. At first it pissed me off, that guy on the news for so many days. But I started to like it when I saw all the different angles. Some weren't so grainy. Now I've got so many different shots on tape, I don't know which one is best. I don't like the ones with blood, I guess. I don't like seeing that big man lying in his blood.

The part I love to watch is when that fat hand swats my fingers from his eyes. There's only one way to learn something, I guess, and that's what happened. I should have checked if he was still breathing, but I didn't. And I wanted those damn eyes closed. But when I look at the video, of all the different angles, I see something else: his eyes are still blinking. Pretty slowly, but I watch at different speeds too.

That's why I left. That blue eye stared right at me and I reached down to close it and he hit me, so I left.

But how else do you learn? I can watch all those shots over again if I want and say to myself, "See, he's still blinking. If someone's blinking, they're not dead." Boom. A lesson. And then I'm out of the shot. I guess I'm walking home.

the underdog

The underdog was drawing water, with that horrible clanging and creaking machine. He was at that terrible well, and paused to put his hair behind his ears. The bucket was too big for him. It was too big for all of us, but he insisted on going. We needed water.

"I'll be careful," he said all the time.

There were snipers all around, in those days. We can't explain it now, but we took it for granted then. He was at that well, and we waited for the crack of a gunshot.

"I'll be careful," he had said. Sure enough, he was.

It's a different kind of care, he would say. Degrees and so on. The care in tying a shoelace, not the care in avoiding moving wheels. The care in not breathing second-hand smoke or wearing very tight briefs, not the care of stooping just under the bullet.

His face was red with exertion and we waited for the air to change sounds—a gunshot, a stop to his laboured breathing. When it did, we imagined the worst, naturally. But it was only that the platform had broken. He was alright but for the broken ankle.

A doctor was sent for. He smiled and sweated. We boiled our tea. We understood.

The ground is soft and wet this morning. The

movies play on. This air is fresh!

We watch the underdog. What will he do now? And we cheer for him silently. He doesn't know he's the underdog.

∞

The preacher's wife was disappointed. Her hair was trim and dark.

"It's a pity we loved him," she said.

Her narrow hips confined her movements to thin arcs, and the gestures of her lips showed us no one knew better. When she continued speaking, and anger sparked in her eyes, the preacher broke out of his meditation, moved to see her as human.

"We have all been misled," he agreed. "Now let's begin the next part. Let's begin to learn what this man is, if he is not an underdog."

∞

In the antique room, with its stale walls beaten full of holes, the air was fresh. It came from outdoors. The underdog sipped tea with us, keeping his ankle carefully elevated, keeping it propped on a pile of rubble. The rubble was on a warm wooden hope chest disfigured by fire.

I looked at the preacher and his wife. He was taking it better than her. The doctor was embarrassed. The gunfire had gone somewhere else, but the signs of the war would not let us believe it was gone forever.

You all think of your roles, I thought, and look at the underdog smile. Look at how tired he is. Look at his missing ear. See his bent ankle and look at its makeshift cast, a tight bandage made stiff by dirt. How has his injury made him less an underdog?

When he fell asleep, or when we heard him snore to prove he was asleep, the doctor could honestly address us all: "Look, I am a doctor," he said. "My job is to make people better. My job is to heal people if I can. I'm sorry."

None of the cowards would admit they cared. I also said nothing.

ↂ

The war is ending and there are trains to catch. A small woman from the city, Lara, speaks to him on the platform. We wince as we see them both smile.

She holds her tiny purse with both hands in front of her, and looks down at her feet. He blushes when she looks up again, catching him in full rapturous stare at a ringlet that falls from her tight pink hat just in front of her ear.

She kisses him on the cheek and whispers her phone number. Specific to the period, nice girls don't do that. She comes from a nice family and she's going nowhere, but enjoys herself. She does nothing wrong, exactly. But when she does right, it's not necessarily on purpose. Is it wrong?

ↂ

I said it in a bar once and it didn't go over very well, except with the preacher's wife. "Sometimes I would like it all to be done with," I said.

Because some of it, honestly, is pure cruelty. There are times when I want it to be over. I want him to be just a figure. Just an idea.

The preacher looked up and said, "We all do," then looked back down at the table. His wife had asked for the car keys hours ago.

"I mean I want sometimes to do it myself," I said. "I want to knock him down. I want to see the stunned look on his face!"

I slammed my glass on the table and took some gum from the pocket of the preacher's wife.

"It's like rubbing a sore," I explained. "Sometimes I can't look at him but I do."

The preacher had his eyes shut and was smiling. His wife took my hand.

"Then when you look up the next time and he's happy or sleeping—" she said.

"You can't help it! You want him beaten and tired!"

We weren't that drunk, the preacher's wife and me. The preacher opened his eyes. He took his wife's other hand. He couldn't believe what he was hearing.

"He's a fine man," he said, mostly to himself. "You want to hurt him?"

Our waitress came by and we sobered up with coffee. The underdog entered, in one of his good moods. I smiled and said hello.

The preacher had enough shame for all of us. The

preacher's wife had her tongue in his ear and I don't think he noticed.

"Off to the movies with Lara!" the underdog said with a wink. His poor red face wanted his body to run, but he walked to the door without skipping.

"She's beautiful," we said, but he was already gone and he already knew.

જી

Free after the war, a survived underdog, the ultimate hero, he went about it all wrong. He did what he could. He muddled through. He eked out a living.

Lara was gone. We knew she would be. She found a man who, if he had ever been less than a hero, hid it extremely well. They loved each other and who's to say?

Things are right for a reason. The green lawn and the sunshine is what we all want. The preacher's wife should never have married him. She wanted a man who would die, she wanted Jesus Christ, she wanted to be a widow, and who can say she was wrong? She cut quite a figure. She worked her way into all of our hearts. The preacher's too—but she would not let him be human, except in his suffering.

જી

The underdog had a crisis of faith years after the war.

"Everyone I know measures themselves against their reaction to me," he said.

"Your excuses for the unfinished house are wearing thin," his wife said, applying a lint brush to the suit on his back. She held the brush up to the window and looked at it in disgust.

"The children cannot see me as their father—"

"Of course you're their father," she said. "I can't believe the way some people—"

"They can't see me as their father," he said, shaking his head.

He turned to face her and she watched him silently, the lint brush still in the air. He walked over to the sink, taking his jacket off and hanging it on a kitchen chair. He turned the tap on and ran himself a glass of water. He held it to the light from the window and waited until the sediment settled and he could see through it clearly. She sat down in the chair his jacket was on and watched his back. A sweat stain was beginning between his shoulder blades.

He drank the water and turned to her.

"My own children pity me," he said.

She shook her head as she rose and walked toward him.

"That was good," he said, and ran more water. "Cold."

She put her arms around him and leaned on his back, clasping her hands around his waist and pulling herself more tightly toward him.

"I loved another woman once," he said.

"I know. Her name was Lara. I knew her. We were friends."

"We all were," he said, setting his glass on the counter and turning to face his wife. His red face trembled. "I have failed at everything I ever tried. My boy pities me and my daughter will as soon as she's old enough."

"They envy you," she said. "Everyone does. Your boy wants to kill you sometimes—that's just how boys are. Your daughter thinks you made this world and everything in it."

"We are all exceptions," he said, hugging her tightly. "But sometimes I feel like . . ."

Tears unrolled from his eyes down his sore face. She kissed him on the cheek.

. . . an archetype, he thought.

ॐ

The underdog was tying ribbons around some neighbourhood trees the last time I saw him. I was on my way to Kinko's for some copies.

"Hi there," he said.

I walked over to the greying man squinting in the sunshine. He needed a rest.

"Good to see you," I said. "What is all this for?"

"Lara's son is one of the hostages," he said, nodding sadly. Then he gave me a hug.

We're all still here. We all still live in this town. He and his wife have a new child. Nobody thought it would happen. There is a home on the outside of town full of people the doctor has saved. The preacher went back to school to be secularized. His wife was secularized as a

baby. I'm plastering the town with posters, asking everyone to reconsider.

the hero comes home

The hero stands on the edge of the bridge, repeating words. We are exactly this frantic, we are precisely this calm, and so on. Stones and pebbles precede him, if he were to fall, or if he were to jump.

The hero has saved the others, the unfortunate, the newscaster says, but what about next time?

In the studio, TV shows may be pre-empted and, more to the point, might she wrap it up?

It's the hero again, someone mutters, not watching. They'll watch later, on the next newscast, or see a clip in a promo.

The hero is tired, make no mistake. He repeats himself on the bridge. Knowing exactly what portion to take and what portion to give. But the rent, and so on. The family and the smiles of the children, say. Even this great river, even this warm weather, even your mother who loves you, or loved you . . .

The preacher's wife calls the preacher. Saving is everyone's business. The preacher will be right there and hold tight, etc.

The hero mentions a name—his name. He is no longer the hero. The preacher's wife is on the phone again. It's up to her, but the preacher could still come.

He is no longer the hero. This is how decisions are made, he says. I have been the hero so long.

A drowning man smiles in the river, glad to have played his part. What a glorious career!

He walked into town to buy the city paper. The ditches ran with muddy spring water and there were wet ruts on the road. Would anyone recognize him?

The preacher saw him a block from the store. How are you? It seemed genuine.

I have so much time, he said. I have all day.
They breathed in the air. They rocked back and forth on their heels.

Ever since I've known you, you've been the preacher, he said. You've smiled a lot. Where does it come from? When will you stop preaching? Am I feeling the same way, now, tired and refreshed, as you've felt all along?

The same old smile. We all have questions.

Mary, he said into the phone.

A woman's voice said hello and then there was silence. Mary, it's me. I've retired. Maybe you've heard.

Mary didn't recognize the voice.

It's me. I was the hero and now I've retired. I've come home. I've been saving people in the city and— Mary, do you still love me?

He concentrated. The phone hurt—it was pressed too hard on his ear. Mary didn't say anything.

The yard outside his window was yellow. Someday

it would all be green, but he saw no hint of change. It was definitely a slow garden. But he felt the peace and the tranquility. It's not as if he didn't know what they were going on about.

"You've got the wrong number."

Mary, is this you?

Sean Johnston was born in Saskatoon and grew up in Asquith, Saskatchewan. He has worked across the prairies as a labourer and surveyor, received a Bachelor of Journalism at Carleton University in Ottawa, and recently finished a MA in Creative Writing at the University of New Brunswick. The manuscript for *A Day Does Not Go By* won New Brunswick's David Adams Richards Award for emerging fiction. Johnston currently lives in Vancouver.

The John Newlove quotation is from the poem "Progress," from *Apology for Absence: Selected Poems 1962–1992* (Porcupine's Quill, 1993).

"There is a Way" was published as "There is a Way to Do This" in *The Malahat Review*; "The Sorts of Things a Man Should Know" in *The Malahat Review* and *Limestone* (UK); "Drowning" and "The Underdog" in *Grain*; "This House" in *Out of Service*; "Prayer" in *Zygote*; "The Saint" and "The Hero Comes Home" in *Geist*.